RARE BIRDS

RARE BIRDS

Edward Riche

Anchor Canada

Doubleday Canada paperback edition published 1997
Anchor Canada paperback edition published 2001

National Library of Canada Cataloguing in Publication Data

Riche, Edward
Rare birds

ISBN 0-385-65862-1

I. Title.

PS8585.I198R37 2001 C813'.54 C2001-900751-5
PR9199.3.R525R37 2001

Cover photograph by John Warden/Tony Stone Images
Cover design by Avril Orloff
Text design by Heather Hodgins
Printed and bound in Canada

Published in Canada by
Anchor Canada, a division of
Random House of Canada Limited

Visit Random House of Canada Limited's website:
www.randomhouse.ca

TRANS 10 9 8 7 6 5 4 3

For Frances

Acknowledgements

Friends too numerous to list offered valuable comment as this book developed. I trust they know who they are and accept my gratitude. I give special thanks to Suzanne DePoe, Peter Gard, Rob Mills and Dick Riche. Kathryn Exner's editorial wisdom made working on the final drafts a pleasure.

There was birch rine, tar twine,
Cherry wine and turpentine,
Jowls and cavalances, ginger beer and tea,
Pig's feet, cat's meat, dumplings boiled in a sheet,
Dandelion and crackies' teeth, at the Kelligrew's Soiree.

From "The Kelligrew's Soiree"

— John Burke

1

As if being unbandaged, coming through gauze, Dave Purcell emerged from a deep trance.

These hazy departures were lately becoming more frequent and of greater duration. Parts of his life were now going unaccounted for, unremembered. He was falling in the forest. Dave calculated, with some dread, that he must have been staring out the kitchen window onto the icy waters of Push Cove for a good three or four minutes, an epic of utter emptiness, before the spell had been broken by the low, dyspeptic growl of Phonse's snowblower coming up the lane to the restaurant.

Dave looked down at the jar containing what would become Phonse's lunch. He unscrewed the lid, removed a layer of waxed paper and studied the cloudy suspension of duck grease. *Confit de canard,* imported at tremendous expense and trouble from Périgord, France, would be Phonse's dinner. Few "lunched" in Newfoundland. They *came to their dinner.*

It was March 31.

Dave had served Phonse the same dish, although with considerably more enthusiasm, a little more than a year ago, and Phonse had declared it "the best bit of duck I ever did eat." If no one else, if none of the fish and chip philistines of St. John's would eat Dave's fare, then why not Phonse. At least he appreciated good food.

It was over the preserved duck with roasted potatoes (tiny, perfect little gems — one blue, one red, one yellow) and a warm salad ("Goat cheese, then! Warm salad, imagine!" Phonse exclaimed in approval) that Dave had made a pact with his neighbor, the extraordinary Mr. Alphonse Murphy — Phonse would keep the lane to the restaurant clear of snow and provide Dave access to his pristine and abundant well water in exchange for lunch on Tuesdays and Thursdays. They toasted the arrangement with a 1982 Pichon-Longueville Comtesse de Lalande. Phonse had slurped like a true connoisseur.

Gingerly pinching them from the jar of fat, Dave laid two plump duck legs in a cast iron pot. He stuck the pot in a hot oven and went looking for a cigarette.

Shuffling through the dining room, he caught his reflection in the mirror behind the bar. There, squeezed between a bottle of Ricard and a bottle of Chartreuse, so that one side of his face was a jaundiced yellow and the other a ghoulish green, Dave was confronted by his rapid decline. His thinning hair, gluey with slumber, was swept up in a cockeyed cowlick, as though the lid to his empty head was flapping open in the breeze. There was five days' growth on his face, foxy patches on his cheeks, thick white spikes around his chin. His wire-rimmed glasses sat crookedly across his nose. He spotted his smokes, crushed in the breast pocket of the oxford shirt in which he had slept.

Green and yellow faced, hair on end, he looked like a villain worthy of challenging Batman. He lit a bent and flattened fag and wondered what evil moniker he would adopt were he to take on the Caped Crusader — the Chef? the Maître d'? No, Dave thought, if anything, he was Fuck-Up Man.

Dave had cashed in the nest egg and sunk all his and his wife's savings into The Auk Dining Room and Inn. Operating a fine restaurant had become Dave's dream. Claire shared the fantasy in the early years of their marriage but it had given way to more practical concerns. Her career as an economist had taken precedence and eventually wings. However unlikely it would have seemed all those years ago, she was now ensconced at the helm of the Palmer Institute, a prestigious and rather right-leaning think tank in Washington, D.C. (Dave had asked if the "tank" was made of some super-strength titanium alloy so as to contain the power of the ideas within), an unromantic twelve hundred miles from the failing restaurant on the outskirts of St. John's, Newfoundland.

The position at the Palmer Institute was a plum. Claire could hardly turn it down; Newfoundland was home to no think tanks and, Dave had to admit, prospects were poor. She had left, not really so suddenly, Dave realized in retrospect, but after a long period of denial, with their future together unresolved. They were to work something out, but phone calls between them were growing less frequent, often terminating quickly after Claire inquired whether Dave had been drinking.

The last three times Dave had seen Claire she was on television, self-assuredly explaining to viewers why the Mexican peso should be radically devalued, why interest rates should be lower and why it was a good thing, a *stability* thing or a *confidence* thing, that most of the world's wealth was in the hands of only twelve families. Perhaps it was an electronic transformation, signals jangled in the ionosphere, waves bent by the gravity of the moon, or maybe it was all the television makeup, but Dave thought her appearance was changing.

Her face had grown taut, her eyes dry and lifeless. (Was she eating properly? he wondered. Her relationship with food had recently gone from one of love to hate. Trying now not the latest restaurant but the latest diet, she told Dave that it was essential to be thin *out there*. It had something to do with *power dynamics*. Did one achieve mastery of the universe by disappearing altogether?) She expressed skepticism with a world-weary smirk. Would he eventually fail to recognize his own wife? Fuck-Up Man strikes again, emerging from the sewers beneath Gotham to destroy a marriage.

Dave had read somewhere of couples who, forced apart, had kept up a sexual relationship over the phone, talking dirty to one another while masturbating. This certainly wasn't possible with Claire, who had grown more sexually inhibited over their last few years. Their lovemaking had started timidly — they were both shy — but evolved into a domain of unrestrained exploration. For a time they fucked often. They fucked anywhere. They fucked in any way they could. After a point, every sexual encounter recalled, for Dave, all those previous. Every taste, every texture against his tongue, every scent, every slippery finger brought back the wonderful smuttiness of the cheap hotel in New York, the mustiness of the friends' hide-a-bed, the dirty and indecent glare of the lights in a toilet. And then one day, the process reversed, memories of sensations past disappeared with each act until the moment itself was gone, seemingly before it happened. Dave would come, but he could not remember having done so, or what it had felt like. Prudish now, Claire would think the suggestion of long-distance mutual self-stimulation disgusting. Considering his scruffy appearance, having slept in the same shirt and track pants for days, Dave thought that telephonic sexual union was likely the only kind of contact any woman would be interested in.

Dave had been indulging himself, but only out of necessity, draining fluids that, left bottled up, would turn rancid and spoil the meat. The act, as erotic as a push-up, now took Dave ages to perform. His imagination could no longer conjure any delicious pictures to hasten ejaculation — gone were the hiked-up smock and parting, plump buttocks of the butcher-shop girls, the starved and dirty mouth of the coat-check matron with her tummy-teasing beehive. The long parade of gossamer gymnasts that once lived in Dave's head had packed up and moved on. The last thing that had truly stirred Dave was a forgotten cantaloupe that had ripened in the light from the kitchen windows. Warmed by the sun, the melon had exuded a perfume that had drawn Dave's hand to give it a searching squeeze. It felt good, somehow familiar, and Dave came close to committing the cook's ultimate crime. Only thoughts of Claire witnessing the disgusting display, happening upon him in the kitchen doing a melon, had brought him to his senses.

Claire. Claire, whose grave prediction about the fate of the Auk was coming true — the venture was a total failure. Chalk up another one for Fuck-Up Man. She was right in every regard. The restaurant was too far from a city with a sinking economy and a population disinclined to enjoy calves' sweetbreads and wine at $150 a bottle. The timing had been all wrong, opening a restaurant in the nineties — the decade of restraint, of moderation. It was all bran and bowel movements these days. A generation was bloated and shamefaced for it. People didn't *drink* any more; they took coffee, went in for creamy concoctions, milkymoccacocoachinos, medicinally flavored with nutty syrups. The baby boomers were scared off the booze and back on the tit. The money was in rehab, not restaurants.

And what nature of demented traveler would visit Newfoundland during the six months of the year it was under a cloak of bitter ice? Claire was right, too, about the name — perhaps it was less than appetizing to remind prospective diners that the chef's forebears had bashed a flightless bird into extinction to fill their pots. "Christ, Dave!" Claire had said. "Why not call it the Beothuk Bar and Grill or the Dodo Arms?"

Dave entered into the venture without the faintest idea of what it took to run a restaurant. Only through trial and much error did he learn to properly cost his menu, to control portioning, to minimize waste, to keep a close eye on pilfering waiters. It quickly became evident that if the small operation was to simply break even, let alone turn a profit, Dave would not be able to hire a full complement of kitchen staff. While he had envisaged being chef, supervising a chef de cuisine and various sous, in the end he alone had to slave over a daily menu of necessarily limited choices. The Department of Health had obliged him to undertake very expensive renovations of the kitchen — hauling up the floor — after his first month of operation. The tiles, it turned out, were not up to code, were a comfortable home for uninvited dinner guests like *Salmonella* and *E.coli*. And Dave did not know the one fundamental truth of the business, the truth that he had, since opening the Auk, heard from every restaurant professional that entered the kitchen to compliment his culinary skills: There is no money in food. Dave got into the racket for the worst possible reason. He just liked to cook.

The Auk was a strict Tudor-revival building with costly post-and-beam construction in accordance with the whims of Claire and her architect brother, the flaming Duncan. (Duncan had chosen the lethal kitchen tiles.) Acquainted only with the mock Tudor of the suburbs, Dave had thought the decision a disastrous one. Never one for an argument, especially with Claire's poorly bred and ambitious siblings, Dave acquiesced. In the end he agreed the building was quite attractive, looking something like an elaborate pastry, a mammoth mille-feuille rising out of the trees. Owing, however, to a lack of anticipated revenue from the restaurant, what was to have been the "Inn" part of the operation remained incomplete. (It was to be an "Inn," a place of rest and wines and a hot meal for the weary traveler, and never a "Bed and Breakfast," a place of poached eggs and tepid tea for the tourist.) Though the exterior was finished, the second story was a hollow, dusty shell. It was so depressing that Dave could no longer bear venturing upstairs. Phonse reported having seen an owl emerge from a vent in the gable. It was probably nesting up there, littering the unfinished floors with the skeletal remains of mice and baby rabbits.

Dave surveyed his domain of failure. The dining room was everything he wanted it to be — nine tables (never an even number!), three of them comfortable, hushed booths against one wall, a zinc bar adjacent to the swinging doors to the kitchen, behind which, with the regular assortment of liquors, was a temperature- and humidity-controlled wine cabinet. The essence of its elegance was its comfort. You could just as easily be in a tony bistro on the Left Bank of the Seine — but for the fifteen-foot-high snowdrift outside the large window on the southern wall.

The dining room was a dismal place in the morning. The dark mahogany wainscoting and the deep olive walls sucked up daylight. It was an evening space, drawing energy only from that warm end of the spectrum issued by lamps and flickering candles. The orange flash from a flambé showed the room's real splendor. Morning in the dining room was always the morning after. The party was over, everyone had gone home.

Dave discovered early that the chemistry of a good restaurant required a critical mass of patrons. If the room was full, a diner could be boisterous, crack jokes, talk loudly without being overheard. Kisses were more easily stolen in a crowd. If just two tables were occupied, on opposite sides of the room, everyone conversed in an awkward whisper. So it was that after the first flush couple of months of the curious, the freebies, the foodies (who dubbed the menu "rustic") and the critics (who raved), the bookings fell off. After another month, the volume of trade slipped below the critical mass and people just stopped coming. There wasn't any point keeping the place up and running for the scattered stray, so Dave advertised that reservations were required. Nobody made them. There were occasional bookings for large parties, but now in Newfoundland's dreariest month of March, the Auk was, for all intents and purposes, shut down. Shut down and Dave shut in. This last storm, a maelstrom of wild white curtains raging southeast from the Labrador, had gone on for the better part of a week. If Dave could still speak, his first words in seventy-two hours would be to Phonse. Phonse, who, judging by the pulse and drone of his giant snowblower, was closing in.

At least Dave could practice speaking with Phonse so that he might not appear to have lost his mind altogether when he went to Larry and Moira's for dinner that evening.

"So, Dave, you must be getting a little cabin fever out there, hey, gah yuck, gah yuck!" Larry would observe.

"Web, Lar' ol' trout, ipth like dis . . ."

Dave had worked with Larry Doyle for ten years at the federal Department of Fisheries. Dave pushed paper in Fish and Fish Product Inspection, Larry in Planning. Larry somehow came to imagine that they were fast friends. Dave toyed with the idea of calling Larry and saying the lane was still snowed in and begging off the invitation. Problem was that Larry was one of those fanatically proud owners of a four-wheel-drive and would insist in coming to the rescue. Larry was the type that relished a good snowstorm so he could jump in "the Four Runner" and take a spin across town for a pack of gum. During Dave's last visit to the Doyles', Larry talked about upgrading, getting a Hummer, a US military machine that could, "seriously, Dave, climb over a fucking brick wall." Dave was sure Larry would do it too, find a brick wall and drive over it in search of a bag of chips.

Dave left Fisheries to start the restaurant. Larry left to become a consultant so that he could sell his services back to the department at double the money and write off the Four Runner.

With the once bountiful fish stocks off Newfoundland now scooped up and split and vacuum-packed and poached and fried to near extinction, owing mostly to the wisdom of many Daves and Larrys, Larry Doyle had become a specialist in something called Retrogression Analysis. Dave found it ethically troubling that Larry could work so long with the department, decrease staff levels so as to create the need for outside consultants, then leave only to return, at a premium, to fill the need. He was pimp, whore and John. Larry had written his own ticket and it drove Dave to distraction.

Claire, on the other hand, admired Larry's initiative. "Look at Larry down there," Claire would say. "He didn't run out and start a restaurant or a fishing camp or open a bookstore. Larry didn't let a midlife crisis screw up his future. He saw where the opportunities were. Larry is not as stupid as he seems, you know, David." How this could be, how someone could not be as stupid as they seemed, puzzled Dave.

He wandered back to the kitchen. Through the window he saw Phonse's big machine, shaking and bucking as it ate into the last drift in the drive. Phonse had built the contraption himself. A great whirling screw — at once denture and churning maw — was mounted precariously on the front of a heavy truck chassis. Two arcs of ductwork, frantically manipulated from Phonse's cockpit by levers, pulleys and cables so that they bobbed like insect antennae, spewed snow to both sides of the machine. The whole assembly was powered by a stuttering, consumptive boat engine.

Dave started peeling potatoes. The tragic charade would soon come down around his ears. In another couple of months the Auk would probably be bankrupt. Claire would finally ask for the divorce and Dave would have to become a consultant like Larry. Thing was, he doubted he could do it. The consultancy field was already crowded with more-eager bloodsuckers than he. The better part of the gibberish and double-talk that was once Dave's stock in trade had now left his consciousness. This might really be the end. Another middle-aged loser biting the dust with nothing but a failed dream that pride demanded he call his *integrity*. This might be the big disaster, the destruction of a man. It was more than just the blizzards of March closing in on him, it was real. Real disaster.

Drink.

A Bloody Mary was a morning drink; good manners, not alcoholism.

Raising a tumbler to his lips, Dave felt the air around him cool. The seal to his snowy crypt was broken. Phonse was in the back porch.

"Judas Priest!" he announced, bursting through the door. "Snow?"

Phonse often made a point with one of these clipped rhetorical questions. Seeing him standing there in oiled canvas, caked head to toe in frozen white gunk, the answer could only be an emphatic *yes*.

"There's a snowdrift, must be twenty feet high, halfway up the drive there, and when the rig tucked into 'er, the pressure, the rush on the expulsion system, must of kicked me back nearly ten feet in a nanosecond, old man! Pressure?" Another question.

"The PSIs had to be incredible. That's two tons of machinery kicked back there, Dave. Snow?" Phonse was vigorously brushing off the heavy coating of sticky, compressed snow regurgitated by the big blower. His boiler suit recalled an aviator's — Commander Richard E. Byrd back from the North Pole, thought Dave. A bushy fur hat of his own manufacture and most certainly made of some creature he had killed, covered a full head of salt-and-pepper crew cut. Phonse claimed to have achieved "eighty-seven percent self-sufficiency, old man." The geezer's energy was boundless, he was always occupied, always on the go.

"Thanks for coming up, Phonse." Dave got out the first words, no problem.

"A Bloody Mary, Dave? Useless, cannot get a buzz until you're chockablock with tomato juice, or *clamato* juice, is it?" Phonse laughed. For Phonse, clamato was funny.

"I've got some *confit de canard* in the oven, Phonse."

"The duck, yes, lovely. Since I ate that here, I've given thought to raising ducks. I swear, Dave, that was the best duck I ever did eat." Phonse was now out of the aviator's suit and standing proudly, erect in his blue overalls of a hundred and one pockets. "The pressure? Judas Priest."

Dave considered Phonse utterly mad and now his best, perhaps his only, true friend in the world.

Once seated, Phonse reached for the bottle of wine sitting between them on the table and struggled with the French name. "Hot Brian, 1978," he pronounced with evident approval through a mouthful of duck.

Doom struck, convinced all was lost, Dave had decided to empty the wine cellar of its treasures. He was determined to keep the likes of a 1978 Haut-Brion out of the receiver's hands. He would drink his revenge on the bank.

"Now, Dave, it occurs to me that you've never been down to the house for dinner. That's not right," Phonse said.

It was true. Though the two buildings Phonse called Central Ops were only a five-minute walk through the woods, Dave had never been inside Phonse's home. The few times Dave strolled down to ask Phonse a question, or simply to take his mind off the Auk's impending bankruptcy, Phonse was outside working on one of his numerous machines. Dave had only seen Phonse's wife,

Debbie, through the veil of a screen door, her sideways glance and crossed arms conveying suspicion, if not outright disapproval.

"It may not be the fancy French gourmet number you're used to, but we'd love to have you tonight."

"Sorry, Phonse. I'm afraid I have a previous commitment."

"Another time, then," said Phonse. "Another time. I'm glad to see you getting out though, Dave. Too long locked away in here and you might go a little wingy, if you know what I mean." Phonse crossed his eyes and stuck out his tongue.

His lunch finished, Phonse leaned back in his chair with the look of a man completely satisfied. He tucked his chin into his chest to squeeze out a rumbling and pleasure-filled belch.

"Dave, old man, with grub like this on the menu, they should be beating the doors down."

Dave filled Phonse's glass, emptying the bottle. The wine's berry purple testified to its youth.

"Really, Phonse, it's looking pretty bad. I'm not sure how much longer this is going to last."

"You should have come up with a Plan B, old man." Phonse dug into a pocket, pulled out a tobacco pouch and deftly rolled a cigarette. "We'll come up with —" Phonse's tongue made a reptilian pass across the glue of the cigarette paper, "— a contingency."

Only the gray hairs on his head betrayed Phonse's fifty-five years; his was the lean physical presence of a much younger man. The impression of youth was compounded by his unwavering optimism. He always had another scheme on the go and though they always sounded utterly ridiculous to Dave, Phonse seemed prosperous enough. Phonse's only worry was his wife Debbie's happiness. She was fifteen years younger than Phonse and he often intimated that she was, with both their daughter and son grown and living on the mainland, becoming restless. To Dave's discomfort, Phonse often talked about his and Debbie's sex life. Phonse reported that she was insatiable. "Dave, old man," he once said, "she's four years from her sexual peak and she's already after lapping me five times."

Dave didn't want to dwell on the fate of the Auk, so he inquired about Phonse's latest project, something Phonse called, in a whisper, the R.S.V. I Prototype. Phonse was so cagey about the project, Dave had never figured out what the R.S.V. actually was.

"Making progress with the R.S.V., Phonse?"

Phonse frowned. He spoke in grave tones. "I'm very close now, Dave, just some pressure tolerance tests left. You want to be very careful at this stage, not get too anxious and forget some little detail. Don't want to be crushed like a peanut. I probably never should have mentioned the project to you, Dave. It's strictly on a need-to-know basis, what-you-don't-know-won't-hurt-you kind of situation on the R.S.V."

"I wouldn't breathe a word, Phonse, on my honor," Dave reassured him.

"I trust you, Dave, I do. It's just that knowledge of a thing like that could be dangerous. Industrial espionage, you know."

Dave liked Phonse too much to laugh at this.

"It's the Winnebago people, Dave. They're the ones that worry me. If anybody is ever here at the restaurant asking unusual questions, no matter how insignificant they may seem to you, you call me." The Winnebago people were a mysterious obsession of Phonse's. Whenever Dave asked his neighbor to explain who they were and what they wanted, Phonse was evasive. Dave gathered that their ways were so fiendish, their intentions so dark, that to speak of them casually was to tempt fate. Dave first supposed that they had something to do with the recreational vehicle maker, but this now seemed unlikely.

"Absolutely, Phonse, if I hear or see anything I'll call immediately," said Dave, rising from his seat. "Now, Phonse, a brandy?"

"Dave, with the cold and the damp running right through me I have to say yes. You wouldn't have a drop of that . . ." Phonse couldn't remember the name.

"Armagnac?" volunteered Dave.

A wide smile spread across Phonse's face. "Yes, Dave," he said, "that, I believe, is the one."

They laughed. Dave fetched two snifters.

Early drinking did not agree with Dave. He felt vaguely ill that afternoon. His head was muddled, as if he had just woken from a poor sleep. If Dave was to become a total ruin, he would have to work on the a.m. boozing, would have to learn to appreciate the beauty of the cantina in the early morning.

Phonse seemed perfectly clear of head on his departure,

having consumed five brandies to Dave's three. The two had laughed at Phonse's sordid stories about the crowd in the nearest village, the town of Push Through, six miles down the road. Phonse told of the suspicious prevalence of the Fitz Flap, the protruding left ear of local Lothario Leo Fitzpatrick, in children of the town; of the fortuitous friction fire (the mortgage rubbing vigorously against an insurance policy) that had consumed Dewey Mercer's store, of the costly lumber reportedly destroyed in the voracious blaze and of fat Dewey's fine new cabin on Sullivan's Pond; of the curious nocturnal comings and goings of the supposedly idle fishing boats of the community. Phonse was born and raised in Push Through, but had left in disgust the very day he finally had the money to buy his plot of land up the road. The short distance separating him from the town constituted a self-imposed exile.

Phonse left to take care of pressing business, something about "the joy juice backing up the line" and the great loss of human life from the resultant explosion if he didn't attend to some pumps immediately.

Dave staggered back to the apartment in the restaurant's basement. The tiny, unused living room and adjoining bedroom were never meant to be a permanent home. He and Claire had planned to buy something big enough in which to raise a family in St. John's. But with Claire in Washington . . .

Over the past few months the apartment had taken on a distinctly masculine odor, which Dave recognized from his days in college, pheromones and farts. Indulging in failure, he let his dirty clothes pile up on the floor. He left the bed unmade. Empty wine bottles that had become ashtrays stood tired guard over his insomnia. To complete the picture of despair Dave always kept the television at the foot of the bed turned on, filling the room with the sickening blue glow of daytime drama and bad news, of boobs and bombs.

He collapsed on the bed (a queen-size model Dave dubbed, due to its lone occupant, the joker). The woman on the weather channel cheerily announced yet more snow for Newfoundland. A massive low-pressure system, a five-hundred-year freak of barometric underachievement, was approaching the island from the southwest, doubling back on its eastward passage so it could pick up more moisture off the cold North Atlantic to dump on old Terra Nova. Luckily, the announcer stated, the area around St. John's would be spared more inches of the white stuff on the ground. They would instead get freezing rain and sleet. Dave laughed. Why not? Things couldn't get any more depressing.

Before the effects of the brandy diminished, Dave made the decision to go to Larry Doyle's in his present state, to forgo the shower and shave and arrive looking a wreck. Doing so would prevent Larry and Moira from later speculating about his condition, whispering in bed about their sad friend's finances, his drinking, wondering whether his failure in the face of his wife's success was an emasculation. It was more dignified to simply admit, with a disgusting public display, that he had undergone a hideous metamorphosis, been transformed by alcoholism, isolation and inadequacy from Dave Purcell into Fuck-Up Man.

The one consolation of dining at the Doyles' was that Moira hated Claire, if only because she envied her. Moira probably secretly wished to leave Larry behind and set out for new horizons herself. Who could blame her? But then, who could blame Claire? It did seem that the men of Dave's generation, having bungled the attempt to become more sensitive, more nurturing, had, in the end, merely disappointed. Did Dave simply want Claire to share his failure, to have kept believing in the dream of the Auk with him so that their hopes could be dashed together? Was that love and marriage? The institution was for better or for worse, certainly. But Dave and Claire had had a civil marriage ceremony at city hall and they hadn't said that part.

Not only was Dave a failure, he was a failure without the power of his convictions. In the end he still had enough foolish pride to put on a brave face for dinner. Sobering up, he decided to clean and groom himself after all, be Dave, the cowardly failure.

He was lying on the bed, and the weather channel lulled him into semiconsciousness. The woman's voice from the television crept into the uncharted regions of his mind. Soon he and the weather lady were shedding clothing. They were going to make love. Weather woman's hot and slender fingers were sliding down his back, her nails delicate talons . . . Dave sat up, suffering the tumescence that Phonse called a chubby.

"The vibrations from the blower, Dave, go right through the seat and straight up your arse. Can't drive her without getting a chub on!" Phonse had reported.

He headed for the shower. As Dave was now considered a professional cook, people who invited him to dinner were always apologizing for the food, no matter how delicious it was. They obviously believed that there was some secret order of gastronomy whose members had incredibly high standards. If the meals in the restaurant were delectable, could you ever imagine what the cook must prepare for himself! Dave thought Moira was among the worst victims of this syndrome. She was a very good cook, the food was always lovely, but her anxiety over the caliber of the meal ruined her evening. After the coffees she was near collapse, just when Larry would start to get stupid from the wine and cognac.

The theory about the cook's own dinner being a sumptuous delight certainly wasn't true in Dave's case. He hadn't made himself a decent meal in months, though looking down at this naked body in the shower there was clear evidence of his consumption of bottled terrines and stinky cheese. A distressing thought crossed his mind: he imagined himself as a kind of incredible sausage, packed to bursting with rich, greasy goodies. He saw himself on the grill, juices boiling beneath his skin, expanding until, with the jab of a monstrous fork, he was mercifully punctured and popped open to drain.

Phonse was right, he needed to get out, even if it was to Larry Doyle's.

2

Dave's decidedly two-wheel-drive Skoda, the world's fastest ashtray, turned the corner on to the Upper Road, which skirted Push Through. The bulk of the houses that constituted the community were on the Lower Road, closer to the sea — about thirty modest clapboard saltboxes and a couple of Georgian monstrosities. With its lights reflecting off the sparkling crust of snow and the glassy water of the cove, with the lazy streaks of smoke from its chimneys, Push Through looked quaint from this distance, something off a Christmas card, certainly not the closed, vengeful rural backwater of Phonse's recollection.

The reported origins of the names Push Cove and Push Through were numerous. Some said it was originally Bushy Bay, and then by some accident of language had become Pushy Bay, then Pushy Cove and finally Push Cove. Another explanation was that the cove had been named after the town, which was situated at the narrowest section of the little bay, or the tickle. Southward-traveling slob ice had to push through the tiny strait as it filled the bay in the spring. Dave witnessed this phenomenon two winters earlier when he was in Push Through buying the land for the Auk. The first ice of the spring was so heavy that it collected in the narrows, forming a dam to subsequent ice traffic. Pressure on the obstruction forced big pans of bluish ice up out of the water, over the beach and into the town's tiny lanes. The Arctic was insinuating itself, knocking on the door.

That cold spring day in Push Through was also the first time Dave set eyes on Alphonse Murphy. The ice barrier had trapped a juvenile humpback whale near the bottom of the cove. The beast had eventually run out of open water where it could surface to breathe and was hopelessly trying to beat its way up through the gathering ice. In doing so it was tearing itself to pieces, slowly bleeding to death in an effort not to drown, filling the air of the cove with a mournful song of desperation. After finalizing the land deal, Dave joined a cluster of bodies on the community wharf who were looking down the cove to where the whale was trapped. The crowd watched a figure walk across the ice, approaching the whale from the shore. The figure stopped near the hole, raised a rifle and fired, in skillfully rapid succession, twelve rounds into the suffering humpback. The reports stretched up the cove, a steady sequence of claps, each followed by a sigh in the wind. The figure headed back to the shore. Someone murmured Phonse's name and the crowd dispersed.

There was nothing quaint about the Upper Road. It was populated by various branches of bad cousins from Push Through, exiled to the bog over generations. Their scattered bungalows and mobile homes, grouped in irrational clusters, were ramshackle. Vicious, mangy curs, a beastly local cross of devious Alsatian and surly husky, piss-patrolled the rusting car wrecks that littered the yards. There did seem to be community spirit of a sort, a unity of purpose; neighbors on the Upper Road were always congregated in one garage or another, usually around an automobile fast on its way to becoming a ruin. At first Dave assumed that these people, standing around scrutinizing the cars while enjoying a bottle of beer, repaired the machines. But now he knew that they brought in perfectly good vehicles and disassembled them to display their skeletons in their yards. It was a holdover from their recent hunter-gatherer phase. "Wilf is great hunter, he have many wrecks."

The crowd down below, in Push Through proper, were mostly brown baggers, so named for the lunch bags they took to their jobs in St. John's. There was a small measure of animosity in the city toward the brown baggers, who enjoyed less-expensive housing, paid very little property tax, got the cable and loudly claimed to be examples of Newfoundland's vanishing yet proud rural way of life.

The route to Larry Doyle's took Dave past his father's house, the suburban dwelling in which he had grown up. Not downtown, but *town* nonetheless. Dave escaped the burbs when he was nineteen to enjoy a brief bohemian phase in the heart of the old city. He and Claire met at one of the hundreds of late-night parties thrown at his old downtown digs — a large Victorian row house, barren of furnishings, close enough to the St. John's harbor that you could smell the salt water and the fetid sewage of ages.

They both ended up at graduate school in Toronto, Dave studying geography, Claire economics. They hooked lucrative and secure government jobs in the late seventies and got married. Just like that.

As the lights of St. John's grew closer, Dave figured it must have been the salad days in Toronto that induced the lunatic notion of operating a restaurant in the brown-bag belt outside town. If he had remained in St. John's he probably wouldn't have been so given to romanticizing. The peculiar little city gripping the steep sides of a small harbor seems magical on first sight. Its streets are a senseless maze, the map of a drunk's progress. Its wooden row houses are painted the most audacious colors to combat the dreary agency of persistent fog and drizzle. The people, the Townies, seem friendly, generous with colorful opinions, spoken with a distinct mongrel brogue of Irish and English influence. They are surprisingly worldly. For the people of the many outports along the coast of Newfoundland, St. John's was Sin City, impossibly cosmopolitan and jaded for such a small place. The charms of St. John's were undeniable, irresistible. No wonder it had suckered so many souls. The people that really lived in St. John's, the ones who hadn't gone away too long or hadn't fallen under its spell during a brief visit, the real Townies, knew better. They could see the old-world weariness in the new, but still smell the wood smoke of the frontier. They knew that St. John's was, beneath the pink and powder blue paint, the political capital of a four-hundred-year legacy of misery and deprivation, a desperate colonial outpost of missed opportunities. Dave's town.

Larry Doyle lived in one of St. John's more desirable neighborhoods, midway between the arty riffraff of the downtown and the dull government clerks of the suburbs. His house backed on Rennie's Mill River, which ran through the city in a verdant little valley. It gave Dave some pleasure to park his battered orange Skoda (with one green door courtesy of Phonse) behind Larry's latest four-wheeler. He hoped it would give the neighbors pause. Screw this demographic, Dave thought, they were supposed to be spending their money in his restaurant.

Dave was greeted by Larry and Moira's odious twins, Damhnait and Sinead. (The Gaelic handles were just one consequence of Larry's uncertain Irishness. Like so many of the St. John's emerald set, Larry had taken the pilgrimage and returned with a faux accent, a dangerously naive soupçon of republican sensibilities and a taste for all that was Eire.) The girls opened the door, squealed, said something smart they had learned at Poopsie's day care for gifted children or full Mandarin/French immersion kindergarten or wherever the hell they were now (Dave knew he was supposed to remember) and waited for Dave to respond. He didn't know what to say or do (was he obliged to tip them?), and so simply stood there forcing a grin. Baring teeth was a miscalculation, for it set the pair to wailing like savages.

Moira, seeing the show had bombed, quickly corralled the girls for bed. Dave knew they had been kept awake for his benefit, Larry imagining that Dave cared. Larry thought that the girls' fit of hysterics was endearing. "The Dynamic Duo!" he said. He thought better of announcing that he was the Caped Crusader's newest and most nefarious enemy, Fuck-Up Man. "Beautiful girls, Larry," he said.

Dave could never say they were hideous, that genetics, that Larry's toxic seed ensured the girls would evolve into monsters. As maladjusted adults, the girls might prove an interesting case study for the nature versus nurture debate — was it rotten DNA or formative years spent listening to their Dad's witless yammering that had so scarred them? The Purcell Quandary they would call it.

Dave and Claire had tried, briefly, to have children. He doubted their inability to reproduce was the result of some physiological problem. Dave put it down to a lack of will on the part of the sperm and egg involved in such uninspired coupling.

Dave gave Larry his coat and agreed to a drink. Moira joined them on the white leather living-room set. She had decorated the house in a retro sixties style. The coffee table had wings suggesting an old Cadillac, the art on the walls was Op. In the subdued lamplight it was a pleasant effect, with just enough irony, enough taste for kitsch, to be unpretentious and therefore comfortable. The furnishings were so appropriate, so true to the age of the house, that parties here recalled for Dave "cocktails" his parents used to throw when he was a kid. Attending fêtes at the Doyles', Dave felt almost as though he were acting out scenes from his parents' lives, playing, with remarkable conviction, at being just as fucked up as they were.

Dave, now studying alcoholism to perfect his ruination, noted the depth of Moira's drink. A full day at work, the twins and preparation of dinner had taken their toll. Moira wore the deep fatigue of motherhood and marriage to an asshole that rest could not relieve. Her triple scotch was analgesic. She used to be so vital, just about crackling with energy, thought Dave, now she's simply beat out.

Larry, of course, was full of noisy enthusiasm, he was brilliant at doing nothing all day long and now, to Dave's horror, billing it to the taxpayer.

Larry inquired about the Auk. "I mean, what's going on, are you closed for the winter or what? I saw the ad in the paper and couldn't make sense of it."

Dave started to explain but was interrupted by Moira.

"Larry, it was perfectly clear! Reservations are required. Jesus, the twins would have understood." Moira's last word was addressed to her whiskey. Booze was such a good listener.

"Yeah," said Dave, thankful for Moira's interjection, "I'm mostly going for large parties until the tourist trade picks up."

"Good thing you've got the rooms upstairs," said Larry. "I mean, going out there this time of year could be tricky, you might end up stranded. But a big party? Could you put them all up if the roads were closed? Did you ever get the upstairs finished?"

Moira stepped in to save Dave again. "We saw Claire on TV the other night."

"Of course, right! I almost forgot," said Larry. "She was on with Kissinger."

"No, Larry," said Moira, too tired to be patient with her husband, "it was some former State Department guy who was saying some bombings somewhere were necessary."

"You sure that wasn't Kissinger?" Larry wondered.

The evening was shaping up worse than Dave had imagined. Questions about the Auk and Claire would probably be launched at him all night. He would have preferred to talk about the twins. He leaned back on the couch, struggling to free some flab that had escaped his shirt and painfully adhered to the leather upholstery. He looked out the bay window, through the leafless trees and onto Rennie's Mill River. It was horrible down there. Through the darkness he could still make out the leaden color of the freezing water, fluid only by virtue of its movement. Every splash stained a rock with ice. Smart people were in the Caribbean somewhere. They would have to eat. They would go to a restaurant, order spicy prawns and juicy local fruit right off the tree. Why had Dave imagined the Auk had even a prayer of succeeding? "Come experience the Ice Age as Cro-Magnon Man experienced it, eat at the Auk! Nuclear Winter? No problem! The soup's on at the Auk."

Larry was telling Dave about the machinations at Fisheries, old office gossip that now meant nothing to Dave.

"Talk about caught with your pants down!" Larry squawked.

Dave was thinking only of the frigid water, of ice, when he spotted something, or someone, skulking through the bushes in Larry's backyard. He squinted to make out who was there. If a burglar was hitting up the neighbors, would he say anything? No, share the wealth, let this local Robin Hood return to his village and shower the cheering poor with pilfered pharmaceuticals, with cellular phones and compact discs, with Nikon and Sony, let this loot-lucky lout do the unholy things with toiletries that burglars were rumored to do. The figure emerged from the shadows. He was dressed in what appeared to be combat fatigues and was approaching the house, brushing branches away from his face.

"Lar?"

Larry kept going. "I mean literally with your pants down, and the minister of fisheries coming through the door. I suppose he was going to jerk off or something."

Not only was the figure closing on the house with purpose, he was carrying something, something against his shoulder. Christ, he was only twenty feet away . . .

"Duck!" screamed Dave, diving for the carpet.

Moira screamed too, though only because at the exact same moment the smoke detector sounded, signaling that some portion of dinner was burning.

Dave's pants were damp. Had he pissed himself? No, it was his drink, tossed in fright, seeping into the plush carpet. He heard distress in the kitchen, the oven door yanked open, agitated heels on the tiles.

Dave looked up. Larry, who had taken shelter behind an armchair, was now forcing a smile, trying to look composed. Dave realized that Larry wasn't seeking cover from the assassin outside but from Dave himself. Larry had obviously determined that his old pal from Fisheries had lost his mind, was a madman with nerves so delicate, so fragile, that he had been thrown into a panic by the piercing shriek of the smoke detector. Other guys from the department had cracked up; now it was Dave's turn.

"What is it, Dave? Perhaps we can help. Moira's got a tub of Xanax upstairs."

"No," said Dave, "there's a guy with a gun in your backyard."

Larry paled. He switched to a loud whisper. "Moira! Moira!" he hissed.

"Shit," responded Moira. "The torte is toast."

"No, Moira," Larry's whisper was loud enough to be heard by the killer, even through the glass of the window. "Somebody's outside with a gun. For Christ's sake, woman, call Neighborhood Watch."

Dave was pulling himself across the carpet with his elbows. He judged that a dash to the Skoda was unwise, he could never get the thing started in time to escape. He would use the awful twins as a human shield and make a dash for it. Halfway across the room he saw Moira's legs, shapelier than he remembered, marching to the window. He clamped his hands over his ears and squeezed shut his eyes. Glass and gory pieces of Moira would be flying across the room in seconds and still Dave could think only of her legs. He wished he had the courage to stand up and save her. It was certainly Larry the killer was after.

But instead of a gunshot he heard Moira huff and then stamp her foot.

"It's a birder, Dave." Moira wasn't amused.

"What?"

"A bird-watcher. An old man. That's not a gun, it's one of those wonky cameras with the big lens. What is it with you guys? Are you on drugs? Did you guys take drugs? Larry? Where did Larry go?"

Dave stood up. He was mortified and now certain that he was, indeed, losing his mind. He was trying to sputter an apology when Larry came running down the stairs, clutching the groggy twins as a shield against the anticipated hail of bullets.

Dinner was ruined. Not only was the torte burnt but the twins, rudely dragged from their beds by their terrified father, were nearly delirious with fright. It took Moira more than an hour to put them back to sleep. At least the time upstairs gave her a chance to cool down. She was very angry with Dave.

Larry kept going over his version of the event (no doubt soon to become "the Dave incident") until he had turned his act of extraordinary cowardice into a heroic effort to rescue the children. "I don't know why, it was just paternal instinct, I guess, all I could think about was the girls. You really gave me a scare, Dave. At first I thought you had lost it, too much time alone or something, and the blast from the smoke detector just pushed you over the edge."

"I'm sorry, okay, Larry? I am very sorry."

Moira was getting ready to forgive. "It is weird," she said, "somebody out in the backyard at this time of the night. I guess if I wasn't used to them I might have panicked too."

Dave saw an opportunity to mount a defense, to blame it on the old man with the camera. "Yeah, it is incredibly strange. What was he doing out there?" he demanded.

"Roe's crested waxwing," Moira answered. Larry nodded.

"What?"

"He's been sitting in a blind out there by the river all day waiting to get a picture of the damn thing," said Larry.

"It was spotted by a bird-watcher three days ago," said Moira. "It's apparently quite rare. Blown in from Greenland or Iceland or somewhere. The first guy that spotted it called CBC Radio, they have that call-in bird show on Saturday mornings, and since then there have been hundreds of these people tromping up and down the valley."

"They're obsessed," continued Larry. "Some of them are out there from dawn to dusk. One of them showed me a drawing of the stupid thing, it didn't look like much . . . like a little bird. I was expecting something more colorful, like a parrot or something."

"Like a parrot, Larry?" Moira was getting saucy.

"Roe's what?" Dave wanted the name again.

"Roe's crested waxwing. How does its call go again? Is it 'Zreeet, zreeet'? I can't remember." Moira was exhausted.

As he drove back to the Auk, Dave thought that at least after the horrible experience at Larry and Moira's he could look forward to some time alone. He needed time to hatch a plan. That evening's episode was changing his thinking. Seeing a nervous breakdown up close, with its paranoia and embarrassment, he decided to abandon his earlier decision to surrender unconditionally to ruin. His situation was critical, calling for immediate action. He would swallow his pride, sell the restaurant at a loss, try to patch things up with Claire, pull himself together and start all over again.

The car wreckers of the Upper Road were still at it. Dave noticed some pushing and shoving going on by one of the garages. Drunken, sloppy violence under the floodlights. Bull baymen in rut, no doubt. He guessed the meadows behind the homes on the Upper Road were lumpy with dismembered bodies. Yes, he thought, I'll be glad to get clear of this, to return to civilization. Toronto was even beginning to look good.

The headlights of the Skoda swept the woods and the lane leading to the Auk. This time it was no camera. The figure his high beams found in the lane was definitely pointing a rifle at Dave. He slammed on the brakes.

When Phonse saw it was the Skoda, he lowered the gun and ran up to the car, gesturing frantically for Dave to roll down his window.

"Christ, Phonse, what in the —"

Phonse put a finger to his lips. He looked deadly serious. "Just go down to the house. You probably scared them off," he whispered. "Wait in the kitchen. Two knocks, pause, then three knocks is me." He scurried into the woods, his finger tight on the trigger of his .303.

There seemed no alternative but to follow his instructions.

Once inside the kitchen Phonse hadn't waited for an offer but demanded a drink. Dave gave him a tumbler of cooking brandy. Phonse walked about the kitchen in circles, frequently going to the window to survey the woods outside. He kept his rifle close, leaning it against the kitchen counter.

The accumulated trauma of the day was beyond the frail limits of Dave's endurance. After quietly fuming at Phonse's madness for a couple of minutes, he was overcome by a delirious fit of laughter. The adrenaline coursing through his system made him high as a kite. He was again drinking heartily with Phonse, listening to the armed man's explanation.

"I was down in the shed, finalizing the land test plans for the R.S.V. I had the scanner on." Instead of listening to the radio for diversion Phonse kept an ear tuned to a police-band scanner, keeping up with activities on the Upper Road. "I hears this funny cross talk. I put the scanner on search and the next thing I know, these guys are on the walkie-talkies, right. They're talking about the fish, and one of them says, 'The fish is still in position.' And another says, 'That's three hours.' Well, Dave, that's exactly how long I'd been in the shed. So I do this test, I turn out the lights like I'm going to leave, and I hear over the scanner, 'This is Orange Two. The Fish is swimming.' I knew it, Dave, man, they're out there, it's the Winnebagos. How could they know? Unless Uri talked."

"Who's Uri?"

"Uri Svetkov, my partner at one point. It's not important."

"Second time I had a gun pointed at me this evening, Phonse."

"What! They were here before? You said you would call me."

As Dave told Phonse the story of the bird-watcher, the preposterous tale took Phonse's mind off the Winnebagos and he managed to relax.

"Roe's crested waxwing?" Phonse wondered out loud. "Are they fit to eat?"

3

Despite everything that had happened the day before, Dave woke feeling wonderful. He had slept better, more deeply, than he had in months. All the excitement, the fear of guns real and imagined, resulted in a physical fatigue, not the withering weariness of worry and melancholy that he had taken to bed as of late.

Knowing that he would sell the restaurant gave Dave a new resolve. Looking over the room from his bed, he decided to clean the place up. It wouldn't do to have a prospective buyer stepping around soiled underwear.

He went upstairs and made coffee. It tasted wonderful.

The last of the storm had passed and the sky was clear. The ice on Push Cove was breaking up. The sun reflecting off the new bed of snow filled the kitchen with light. A set of copper mixing bowls on the counter were ablaze with the warm colors of an oven. The knives sparkled.

Through the kitchen window Dave saw Phonse approaching. A night's rest (if Phonse ever did sleep) had not improved his outlook. No doubt he was still ruminating over the intrusion of the alleged spies, the Winnebagos. Dave had a cup of coffee waiting for his perturbed neighbor.

"Ahhh," Phonse said with satisfaction, "the real coffee." He didn't bother to get out of his aviator's suit.

"Satisfied that everything's hunky-dory, Phonse?" asked Dave.

"I was just going to check, Dave. Survey the perimeter. I thought you might want to come along with me."

"I could certainly use the fresh air. I think I will."

Between the kitchen at the rear of the building and Push Cove was a hill that sloped steeply to the sea. Rocky and brutally windswept, it could support only deformed dwarfish shrubs, blown flat by the gales off the water, and the scattered patch of blueberry or partridgeberry. In the winter it was icy and treacherous. Otherwise, the restaurant was surrounded by the typically gnarled and wind-stunted coniferous growth that satisfied Newfoundlanders as *the woods*. Dave's only safe access to the ocean was via the many ancient trails that ran through the surrounding woods. To get to the small beach nearest the restaurant, he had to first walk to Phonse's and then down a narrow path to the sea. Near the bottom of the path there was a decaying, sea-bleached slipway, suggesting the area had been settled years earlier. No one could really remember who had lived here, but the crowd from Push Through said it was a solitary and fanatically religious family of Irish immigrants. The story went that the father of the family, instructed by malevolent spirits (devious fairies or the like), murdered his wife and six children in their beds, split and salted them like cod fish, cannibalized them over the winter (With hardtack or potatoes on the side? Dave could not help but wonder) and then disappeared into the woods in the spring, never to be seen again. It was in these woods that Phonse led the search.

Dave seriously doubted they would find evidence of anything more than rabbit traffic, but he enjoyed the bright, cold air. It was, as they said in St. John's, "a clever day."

It was difficult going. The snow was thigh-deep in places and softened to a slushy consistency by the rare sun. Dave bobbed and weaved through the crooked congregation of spruce, grabbing at branches to steady himself. Twice one of his legs sank to his crotch and he had to struggle, to the point of working up a sweat, to free himself. Phonse navigated with considerably more ease.

Buoyant from the crisp air filling his lungs, Dave laughed at the previous night's exploits. "Christ," he said between puffs and pants, "what an asshole I am. I'm going to have to send Moira flowers or something."

"I must say though, Dave, I'm impressed that you spotted the geezer out in your friends' yard," said Phonse, inspecting a broken branch. "Keep your eyes open."

"Roe's crested waxwing," said Dave, laughing again.

"I get the feeling, Dave, that you don't believe there were people watching us last night." Phonse stopped and looked back over his shoulder at Dave.

"No, Phonse . . . well, yes, actually I do doubt it." Dave still hadn't found his breath and Phonse was on the move again. "Not that . . . not that I think you're wrong to worry.

But you could have heard anything on that scanner. I'm a terrific believer in lamentable coincidence."

"True enough, Dave, but how do you explain this?"

They were in an open area where the snow had been packed down by human activity. Footprints were discernible, now rising up from the melting snow like stalagmites, leading from the clearing and heading toward the road. Phonse bent down and picked up a cigarette butt.

"Now then!"

Dave was perplexed. *Had* someone been watching the restaurant? His mood took a dip. There seemed to be trouble in this and, if only because of his recent streak of bad luck, he worried that it would, in the end, become his trouble. He tried to present another assessment of the evidence.

"It could have been anybody, Phonse!"

Phonse looked pleased with himself for having alarmed Dave. "Like?"

"Rabbit hunters."

"Season's long closed. Besides, I heard no gunshots or dogs, don't see no shells," Phonse observed, raising his eyebrows as if asking Dave to present another theory.

"Then the crowd from the Upper Road, checking out the restaurant."

"I'm sorry to tell you this, Dave, but the crowd up there are not particularly interested in fine dining."

"No, I meant casing the place, planning a break-in."

"I would have heard about that."

"You know them?" This was news to Dave.

"We have an arrangement. They know they would have Alphonse Murphy to answer to if they ever knocked over the Auk," said Phonse proudly.

There was some comfort in this. Dave lit a cigarette and tried to give the matter sober consideration.

"Well, Phonse, I guess we should be concerned." The smoke found his lungs tender from the rare exercise.

"Concerned! Concerned! Dave, old man, the boys are on to me. It's the Winnebagos! It's all got to do with the R.S.V."

"Phonse, I don't really fully understand what you mean by the Winnebagos and, to be perfectly honest, I've got no idea what the R.S.V. is all about."

Phonse nodded. His expression conceded that it was unfair to expect poor Dave to fully appreciate what was going on. "Well, you're obviously involved now, Dave, and I'm sorry about that. I truly am. I'm going to come clean. You come down to the house for supper tonight and I'll explain everything."

Dave agreed.

"Great! I'll get back and tell Debbie. Her younger sister's down for a visit. Lovely woman, Alice, you'll like her."

Phonse tromped off. Dave stayed behind, pensively puffing his cigarette, slowly sinking in the snow. He didn't need to be spooked like this now. He had made bold decisions to extricate himself from the mire his life at the Auk had become. There was something about this new wrinkle that promised to set the plan on its ear. Nothing involving Phonse was simple. But he felt he had to accept the invitation. Perhaps during dinner he would announce his intention to sell the restaurant.

He looked up. The sky was losing its luster, quickly turning gray, perhaps bringing a new storm. He couldn't be sure, for he hadn't watched the weather channel last night. He had simply fallen asleep.

A message was waiting for Dave on the answering machine in the apartment. Larry Doyle demanding that Dave never again darken his doorstep? He pushed the button. It was Claire.

"Damn these things all to hell, David. I'm not going to go into it on tape. It's important that you call me, there are things we absolutely must talk about . . . you know that . . . well anyway, call me. We have to deal with this. Shit, I've got another call coming through. Oh! I heard that Larry and Moira are having some problems. Do you know anything? Call me."

She hadn't said "I love you," thought Dave. There was no "I hope you're well." No "I miss you." It was over, she wanted a divorce.

Dave headed off to fetch a bottle of wine to take to dinner.

The wine cellar beneath the Auk was a minor triumph. Its walls were slabs of locally quarried purple and gray slate. Custom-made iron racks tilted the treasured bottles just so slightly forward, keeping the corks damp, and providing the serious scholar a view of the labels. The names read like a sacred text: Gloria, Barca Velha, Sfursat; some only to be spoken in a hushed prayer — La Turque, Le Chambertin, Échezeaux, d'Yquem and, Dave's most cherished prize, a case of the rare and expensive dark ruby 1985 La Tâche. It was tragic that market hysteria had now priced the fermented juice out of Dave's reach. The advent of glossy wine publications, with their product pornography, had set loose a frenzy of conspicuous consumption. People now thought of the damn stuff as an investment.

Imagining the Auk would be his life's work, he had stocked the dusty cellar to last into the next century. The iron workers who fashioned the racks threw a crude iron table and chair into the bargain. When the cellar was illuminated by candlelight, the sense of reverence for the grape was total. Dave noticed, and thought it appropriate, that visitors always whispered in this holy place. Having the passion of any true collector, Dave was satisfied to simply study his cherished bottles for hours on end. These meditations were a strangely masochistic act. There was no region of Dave's memory dedicated to the sense of taste. Music could be elicited and hummed, pictures could be drawn against closed eyelids, but no amount of tongue rolling and lip smacking could call back sour cherries or salt fish or candied apple. While the profound black currant essence of a Ridge Montebello was familiar in every new bottle opened, taste remained the sense of the present, the command to continue living.

But with the message from Claire on his mind, he immediately reached for and opened an unremarkable California Cab. Dispensing with any study or appreciation of the wine's color or aroma, he poured and drank carelessly.

Dave lit a candle on the table and slumped in the chair. This cellar had been for Claire too, she had been the first to bring home a good bottle of wine, to buy something other than an affordable and dubious Chianti. They were to have retired early, turned the Auk into a private retreat and drunk their way through the treasures around him. Some bottles, like the golden d'Yquem and a few ports, wouldn't even be ready until the blissful couple would have been in their sixties.

He decided to pull it together too late. Jesus, it was over. It was all over so soon. The way things were going, he could expect to be shot down dead by the evil agents of Winnebago when he walked out the door, a victim of lamentable coincidence, of his assumed knowledge of Phonse's R.S.V. He needed to fend off the demons of dejection, struggle free of the despair that had been tossing him so carelessly about. Better to go down fighting, to hit the turf with a defiant grin. He stood and reached for two bottles of the La Tâche. Perhaps they were, at eleven years of age, a little young, but tonight Dave was not.

Dave felt a little self-conscious for having worn a jacket to dinner. He was thankful he had forgone a tie. All the same, the gesture seemed to amuse, even charm his hosts. He realized that this was the first time in their acquaintance that he had seen Phonse out of his overalls. He greeted Dave at the door wearing a T-shirt that showed off a lean but fiercely muscled frame.

Having seen only her scowl through the screen door, Dave was pleasantly surprised to find Debbie smiling and laughing. She gestured with a broad swing of her arm for Dave to come in. She too was the very picture of strength, slightly taller and broader than Phonse, but still tightly muscled. Even her hair, an immense black tangle, seemed to struggle against the restraint of the elastic tying it back. Her ample breasts pushed forward with the same vigor. It was Phonse's fault, but Dave couldn't help but think of her with her clothes off, marching toward a bed with hungry determination.

There in the porch they seemed like the oldest of friends, like family. Dave was slapped on the back as if he were the prodigal son.

Dave was taking off his boots when Debbie's sister, Alice, came out of the kitchen to be introduced. She held a heavily thumbed paperback. Dave noted the title — Continental Drift — imagining it might help him divine this woman's character. She must have been five years younger than Debbie, in her mid-thirties, Dave guessed. She was made of more refined stuff than her big sister. Her movements were more languid. Even her reflex of blinking was reduced to a deliberate lifting and dropping of the lids. It startled Dave how long she could leave them closed, and how surprisingly green the iris was each time she carefully revealed them. Alice had attacked her thick auburn hair with less mercy than Debbie, cutting it quite short. The style flattered the sharp line of her jaw and accented a wide mouth. Her skin was paler, had seen less of the sun, than her older sister's, fair enough to show faint freckles high on her cheeks.

"So, you are the famous Dave," she said, extending her hand.

Dave reached to out to meet her grasp, but Alice was covering her mouth to suppress a yawn.

Dave sat with Phonse in the front room of the house. It was cozy and comfortable, with a well-worn, overstuffed couch covered by a crocheted throw. Mismatched armchairs pointed toward a large console television in the corner. The house was toasty warm. An incense of wood smoke mingled with the aroma of roasting meat.

"Smells lovely, Phonse."

"Caribou. The last of the one I got last winter. I has the moose license, right!" Dave had heard this story before but wanted to hear it again. "And my brother Donny has the Caribou license. We split up and I takes the shot and down goes Mr. Caribou. Then I hears another shot, Jesus! I figure Donny's after shooting one too, right? I runs back. He got the moose!" Phonse smiled broadly. "You get the license yet?"

Dave had applied for a moose license on Phonse's behalf, Phonse not being eligible to receive one two years in a row. Phonse would shoot the animal, attach the appropriate tags to the dead creature and give Dave a hindquarter. The procedure of getting the license had entailed Dave meeting certain qualifications on a shooting range after several weeks' instruction in marksmanship from Phonse, firing at bobbing bleach bottles from the old slipway.

Phonse had presented Dave with a fine old 12-gauge shotgun for his troubles. The weapon now leaned against the wine cellar wall, needing oil, gathering dust. The blaring experience of the shooting range was enough for Dave. He didn't think he could put a bullet in anything more vital than a paper target. Dave's father and his brother, Lloyd, were passionate hunters, into the woods, full of cheery blood lust, as soon as the peaty earth chilled firm every fall. Dave joined them on a couple of trips, feeling somehow that he should, that it was his heritage, something every good Newfoundlander did. He could stomach the bird hunting — the killing of ducks and partridge — but found himself genuinely distressed at the sight of big game expiring. It wasn't always so. As a boy he thrilled to the sight of blood, was excited by a kitchen floor covered in dead seabirds, turrs and puffins and bull birds waiting to be plucked. No pleasure had matched accompanying his father to the St. John's waterfront in the spring of the year to buy seal meat. The sealers were big, strapping men — ice-dancing giants, stained-blood filthy and scented-fat rancid from hundreds of kills. Young Dave thought these men a superior breed, the perfect measure of courage and dignity.

On the last hunting trip Dave joined, at least fifteen years ago, his father had bagged a cow moose, shot it cleanly from twenty yards. The creature was staggered by the bullet, its legs buckled, but it regained its footing and trotted, drunkenly, into a grove of trees. After the shot, Dave's father sat on the ground and casually lit a cigarette. "She's dead," he explained calmly. "Square in the lungs." They waited a few minutes before following the bloody trail. They found the cow on its side, its labored breathing spraying scarlet mist. Dave's father shot it again, in the head, and the great beast was dead, its dumb animal eye fixed on Dave.

"No, Phonse, no tags yet."

"You put in for the Gambo area? Any sex?" asked Phonse.

"Yes." Dave reassured him that he had fully understood the specifics of the license application. Phonse was anxious that he not be without a freezer full of moose and had already checked these details with Dave a dozen times. Dave also knew, without looking, that there was a pantry full of bottled moose, rabbit, caribou and partridge off Phonse's kitchen. He knew because the house, its smells, its warmth and wear recalled his maternal grandmother's out in Notre Dame Bay. He hadn't visited those people in years and now, so at home in Phonse's front room, achingly wondered why.

Dave held up the two bottles of wine. "I should open these . . ."

"Let them breathe, hey?" Phonse finished for him, smiling.

Phonse was obviously proud of the knowledge of wines he had acquired at Dave's. Sitting at dinner, he swirled the La Tâche in the glass (Dave figured he must have bought a good set of wine glasses only recently), he sniffed thoughtfully, swirled again, sniffed again, sipped, considered, sipped again, squinted at the purple juice, drew air over his tongue and sipped again before pronouncing the La Tâche extraordinary.

"Ever had a glass of wine like that, Deb?"

She had made faces, mocking his affectation, as Phonse played the sophisticated oenophile. "It's lovely, Dave, lovely wine," she responded.

"A meal like this deserves the very best wine," said

Dave. It was true. The caribou was the most succulent game he had ever tasted, delicate meat with a faint taste of the woods, hints of spruce and lichen. It was served with a concentrated dark gravy, accenting the stronger elements of the meat and of onion. The secret, Dave knew, was the salt pork fat in which the caribou had been seared. The slightly sour, slightly briny renderings of the fatback brought out the deepest reserves of the meat's flavor. Dave thought he could eat the gravy with a spoon. The caribou, with miniature potatoes and carrots burnished in the rough soil of Phonse's garden, had been slowly oven-braised under a thick and fluffy biscuit pastry. Debbie's caribou pie!

Dave sopped up some gravy with a piece of the pastry. He followed a mouthful of caribou with a sip of the La Tâche. They were, though of such far-flung origins, meant to be together.

Sun-baked raspberries came out of the wine, a tease of anise, a buttery suggestion of toasted oak. There was leather in the perfume and, as with any great Burgundy, a muted note of manure.

"Phonse is becoming a regular connoisseur," Dave told Debbie. Phonse fluttered his eyelashes at his wife.

"It's just wine, though, all the same," said Alice.

Phonse took umbrage. "My dear, this is some of the finest wine in the world. But then, what would you, a woman from Gull Tickle, know about —"

Dave laughed. "Yes, it's only wine," he said. "That's all it's supposed to be. But do you like it?"

Alice picked up the glass in front of her. Mimicking

Phonse, she swirled and sniffed. She brought the wine to her lips, looking over the glass toward Dave with glee in her eyes. As she sipped the wine her eyes closed. She replaced the glass on the table without opening them. After serious consideration she looked back at Dave. A broad, slightly bucktoothed smile crossed her face. "Lovely bouquet," she began, "glorious pinot fruit, naturally. Oddly a little cigar box . . . tobacco and cedar. It's evocative, recalling a groomed hardwood forest, losing one's cherry and a prized truffle pig, while rolling around in the shade of a majestic —"

"Al-las!" said Debbie.

"Don't mind that, Dave," said Phonse. "She's saucy by nature."

Dave sensed his neck reddening.

"Seriously, Dave, it's beautiful," Alice said, her tone turning from mockery to warm accord. She looked into his eyes. "Just about the most beautiful thing I've ever tasted."

Dave's pulse was racing, the sting of humiliation was suddenly a playful and strangely pleasurable slap. Still Alice was looking him straight in the eye. Dave felt as though he were being hypnotized.

"Alice is in here looking for work," Phonse volunteered coolly.

Alice's eyes dropped to her plate, releasing Dave.

"Sorry, what, Phonse?" Dave found himself giddy, short of breath.

"She's looking for a job. The fish plant in Garnish is closed. No sense looking for anything there."

Alice rolled her eyes. She wasn't interested in cutting fish.

"Well, best of luck," said Dave, turning back to his meal. "Too bad my restaurant isn't up and running, I could probably have given you something, waitress, what have you." Dave looked at Debbie as he spoke. Debbie smiled back.

"Things will pick up in the summer," she said.

It seemed to Dave that both Phonse and Debbie had noticed the profound effect Alice had on their neighbor. He thought they had shot one another some kind of look, and felt faintly embarrassed.

The dessert, a blueberry duff, equaled the caribou pie.

Dave offered to help with the dishes but was shooed off by Debbie and Alice. It was unthinkable that the guest should do anything but loosen his belt, put his feet up, relax and enjoy himself. Dave was disappointed. He realized he wanted to be in Alice's company. The woman stirred long-dormant feelings in him. He supposed that any attractive woman might have, it was so long since he had been laid. Rather than make Alice uncomfortable with his perverse attention, he had avoided her eye after the brief episode of hypnotism. Now he worried that his feigned lack of interest would be mistaken for rudeness or, worse, disinterest.

Phonse suggested, in a whisper, that they go to his work shed so that he could finally elucidate the R.S.V. matter. Dave agreed and started for the front door.

"No, no, Dave. We'll take the tunnel."

If Dave had needed any more proof that Phonse was not entirely sane, it was found in the tunnel. Phonse led Dave down a set of narrow stairs to the basement. He marched to the far wall and proudly opened a door disguised as a wall panel. He preceded Dave into a cramped passage. Dave had to crouch slightly but could see that the tunnel was well reinforced with thick posts and beams. It seemed safe and was exceptionally well lit. At one point his arm touched a hot water pipe running the length of the tunnel. Dave looked at the pipe and was astonished to detect changes in the pattern of the patina on the copper pipe. From moment to moment, as the hot water ran through the pipe, waves of electric blue and church-steeple green and flashes of brandy orange migrated across the surface. Beneath it was another pipe containing cold water, decorated with tiny dancing beads of condensation. How could he see such minute detail? Dave felt a feather tickling the roof of his mouth, a metallic taste of LSD on his tongue he recalled from his university days.

It was the lights.

The walls of the tunnel were alive. Under these lights Dave could see minuscule living fibers squirming in the tightly packed earth, tiny organisms making the dirt vibrate. He held his hand in front of his face and was able to peer down the pores of its flesh. The hairs on his hand were swaying gently at the command of otherwise undetectable air currents. Dave looked at one of the three lights hanging from the walls. They were each perfect luminous squares. And while they gave off light of a most extraordinary intensity and quality, Dave could stare directly into them without even the slightest discomfort.

"This is something else, Phonse."

"A convenience originally, Dave, but now, with the woods crawling with the Winnebagos, an absolute necessity. Come on."

"No, not the tunnel. The lights. I've never seen anything —"

"Svetkov lamps. The Uri Svetkov Illumination System. Remind me to tell you all about it. Great story."

"How do they work?" Dave wanted one of these lights.

"It's truly a mystery to me, Dave. They draw very little power. You can light the biggest kind of room with a double A battery. It's got something to do with pulses, different frequencies mixing it up, wave patterns. Now, Dave, my friend, I am not unfamiliar with your basic electronics, but the workings of those lamps is scientific hocus-pocus. Strangest thing about it, though, you can't read with them. Whatever it is about the light, the letters on the page just float right off the paper. It's the wildest thing you ever did see, drive you right off your head. They're great for the tunnel but kind of useless anywhere you might need to do any reading or study some plans."

They came to the end of the tunnel and walked up a set of steep wooden ship's stairs to the shed.

Phonse had managed to fill the vast space with tools and machinery. There was an enormous lathe, a couple of drill presses, welding equipment umbilically attached to tanks of acetylene. There were puncheon tubs and coils of thick rope, winches and gaffs. It was heated by a stout old iron stove. The place smelled of tarry smoke and brine-soured timbers. Electronic devices, voltmeters and whatnot, their housings cracked and their wiring exposed, were strewn carelessly about. What appeared to be a small boat covered with a mottled tarpaulin was suspended by heavy cables from the high ceiling at the room's center. Hand tools and litter on the oil-glossed concrete floor beneath the shrouded vessel suggested that this was Phonse's latest project.

Dave couldn't change a washer, couldn't nail two boards together, and so admired self-reliant types like Phonse. He wanted to be like them, one of the boys. As he surveyed the space, Phonse fetched a bottle of dark rum and poured generous measures into two filthy glasses. No mix was offered.

"Now, Dave," said Phonse, "before we get down to business, I would like your opinion on something."

"Sure, Phonse," said Dave.

"You've been around, hey, Dave?"

"Yes."

"You're a man of the world, you've spent a few years in the big city, hey?"

"Yes."

"I don't mean to imply anything." Phonse was shifting from foot to foot, massaging the back of his neck. He seemed unable to get the question out. "And I'm not suggesting that you would have any intimate knowledge of . . ."

"What, Phonse?" Dave was becoming impatient. The first sip of petroleum-scented rum was burning his guts. Phonse shuffled about ten feet away to a small heap, also covered with a tarpaulin. He hesitated, then dramatically pulled off the wrap. It was simply a small, tightly bound bale of something, wrapped in canvas.

"What is the question, Phonse?"

"I found this . . . salvaged it, sort of . . . I noticed an operation . . . yes, an operation being undertaken at sea, there were at least twenty more like this one." Phonse drew a deep breath. "What I want to know, Dave, is whether this is the cocaine or the heroin?"

Dave took a long drink of rum. He was speechless.

"Not that I'm a drug addict, or planning on becoming one, but it must be worth a few dollars," Phonse added.

A terrifying realization came to Dave. He grabbed Phonse hard by the arm.

"Christ in heaven, Phonse, that's who's been watching you, it's the cops!"

"No way, Dave, I recovered this booty over two years ago. Haven't told another soul. Besides, the boys got the rest of it out, no problem. It's not uncommon, you know, Dave, there's all measure of funny business going on these days. Can't fish."

Dave knew this to be true, that the enterprising brigands of the bay had turned to clandestine activities to fill their pockets and their time. He had tried deciphering various winks and nods directed his way in Push Through, but the exact nature of the goings-on had never been revealed. Dave was still an outsider to the people in the area, not privy to the many murky secrets of Push Cove.

"It's . . . Jesus, it must be . . ." Dave was thinking of bolting.

"It's twenty-six pounds," Phonse said, looking at the bale. He was suddenly very nonchalant.

"Christ, Phonse. What do you want *me* to do?" Dave heard the pitch of his voice rising.

"Tell me what it is? How much it's worth? Where to unload it? I mean, have you ever tried cocaine?"

Dave figured it was best that he lie to Phonse. He

had, in fact, tried cocaine on a couple of occasions. Larry had acquired it somewhere. It had been a naughty little thrill during one of the Doyles' dinner parties. Larry and Dave sneaking off to the bathroom, snorting a couple of lines off the flush box, returning, all chatty, to the other guests and finding them suddenly interesting. But Dave was glad not to know where Larry had purchased the powder, for he found the stimulant compelling enough to suffer an all-nighter at his colleague's kitchen table, listening to the bullshit until all of the drug was gone. The stuff gave him dangerous opinions and the bravado of Mr. Hyde. He knew he should lie, plead ignorance.

"Well . . . yes, I have tried it a couple of times, but . . ."

Phonse clapped his hands together with glee and opened the bale. Kerosene fumes wafted through the air. "So?" he asked.

Dave tiptoed toward the bale. Inside was an enormous quantity of sticky off-white powder. He couldn't guess how much it represented, having seen only small amounts, portions of a single gram. The powder was composed of billions of tiny crystals that flashed white and blue and even pink. The twinkling drug set his nerves tingling with alarm. He felt he was at the center of some great crime.

"I don't think I can tell by just looking at it. For Christ's sake, Phonse, I'm no expert. Just throw the stuff in the bay. People will kill for this stuff. Jesus, if the cops —"

"You mean it doesn't look like cocaine?" Phonse asked, disappointed.

"I don't know, Phonse!"

"Calm down, Dave, old man. How are we supposed to know what it is, then?"

Dave noted with discomfort that Phonse had switched to *we*.

"I could taste it, I suppose." Dave knew he should never have said this.

Phonse was surprised. "With your mouth?"

Dave licked his index finger, stuck it into the bale and rubbed a sample of the powder on his gums. He didn't know what this would prove, only that they did it in the movies.

"I thought you put it up your nose," said Phonse.

Dave's teeth seemed to disappear and the roof of his mouth was quickly following them to never-never land.

"Yes, Phonse, it is cocaine and you do put it up your nose."

"Is it any good?"

Dave laid down his drink. Why was he making this mistake? he wondered. He pulled a key from his pocket, scooped up some of the cocaine and laid it on the top of a barrel. Phonse was studying him closely. Dave carelessly crushed the powder into a finer state, leaving portions of it in chunky, rocky, nasal-membrane-chewing bits. He withdrew a five-dollar bill from his wallet, rolled it into a straw, bent over and sucked a greedy helping up his nose, making the mistake.

His heart started to pound heavily, his jaw grew steely. He ground his teeth and wondered what the setup was here. Perhaps Phonse was with the police and they were trying to pin some long unsolved drug crime on him. In Dave's time cocaine had become very bad stuff. A barometer of the culture's mood swing from one of license to one of penitence, it now marked a dark zone in the North American imagination. Once a glamorous diversion for rock musicians and movie stars, harmless enough to be dubbed *nose candy*, it had been reinterpreted of late by drug czars, fighting a crusade against thin, mustached Latino drug lords whose ultimate objective was to ruin America, turn the United States into a nation of crack babies. The drug meant sleeplessness, paranoia, violence, abandonment of responsibility, moral turpitude.

Perhaps Claire was behind it all, paint him a drug addict so she could clean him out in a divorce settlement. It wasn't such a stretch, Dave had the junky look. Who was she to criticize, topped up on her "I wouldn't have a career without it" Prozac? Was it still Prozac or hadn't she moved on to a more refined, more precise agent, one designed to help you forget your wretched husband and get on with your life, the *über* serotonin re-uptake inhibitor. Prozac, thought Dave, Zac, Z, and decided that all substances whose names contained the letter *z* were sinister. There was a plot by a league of deranged pharmademons, working away in their secret alpine laboratories, concocting Zyparex, the pill that lets you forget your parents; Zoslag, the pill that made you love your job; Zafomor, the pill that made you famous; Zerothon, the pill that made it all go away. Perhaps her pills did have the rumored, homicidal side effects. Maybe Claire planned to have him killed. He was in a terrible panic. What was he putting up his nose? Who could Phonse be working for?

Was he mad? Phonse wasn't working for anybody. He was the best chap Dave ever had the pleasure of knowing, certainly a thousand times more interesting and genuine than any of the morons he had known at Fisheries. His days with Phonse had been the best of his life. Jesus! He loved it out here. He was free.

"It's good, Phonse. The best I've ever had."

"Yes, then!"

Dave had to try more.

"Watch it, Phonse, if you ever do this stuff, watch it. It's pure, I think. Take more than a gram and a half and you are a dead man."

"Wouldn't think of touching it," Phonse said. Dave thought this might be a slight reprimand, but Phonse continued, "You help yourself, though. Go mad."

Dave calculated that his last line had been too meager so he had another. It all seemed so funny.

But they had come to the shed so that Phonse could offer some explanation of the R.S.V. What did the cocaine have to do with it? Was R.S.V. hip street lingo for the substance? Was it a particularly sought-after variety of the drug, rendered from coca leaves harvested in some remote Andean valley blessed by Inca gods?

"Phonse, I still don't understand what R.S.V. means, and why would these Winnebago people be interested in this . . . this . . ." Dave laughed out loud. "*This giant sack of blow!*" He buckled over.

Phonse was taking note of the effects of cocaine. They seemed agreeable.

"It's an entirely unrelated matter, old man. This . . ." Phonse walked toward the large mass suspended from the ceiling and pulled off the heavy tarpaulin. "This, Dave, my friend, is the R.S.V. I Prototype."

Surely the drugs had something to do with the vision. Before Dave, propped up on two carefully padded wooden braces, secured by heavy cables, was a lustrous black fifteen-foot metal cigar.

"This," Phonse continued, "is a prototype of a Recreational Submarine Vehicle." It did indeed look like a submarine. "Or R.S.V. for short."

Dave took some more cocaine. (So the Winnebago people really were with Winnebago.) "Phonse," he said, "it's extraordinary."

4

The design for the miniature submarine had come to Phonse through Uri Svetkov, the brains behind the Svetkov Illumination System. Svetkov was a Bulgarian who had boarded at the Murphy house. He was among the thousands of refugees from the crumbling Soviet Bloc that had poured into Newfoundland during the early 1990s. Foggy Newfoundland — not their choice — had been their only opportunity to defect as Aeroflot's Cuban-bound flights refueled at Gander Airport. Phonse reported that Uri was particularly disappointed in Newfoundland, having imagined democracy looking a lot more like Southern California: sunny and prosperous, lady liberty an easy blonde with jiggling tits on Rollerblades.

When his application for refugee status was rejected (Uri had told the review board that he planned to continue his work in eugenics in the new world), the Bulgarian fled.

"I figure he set out for California and that's where the boys from Winnebago got wind of him and the R.S.V."

Rum and cocaine were making Dave very high. He was loving the story. "I wonder, though, Phonse, if there's a very big market for recreational submarines."

"Roe's crested waxwing, my friend, that's all I have to say to you." Dave didn't make the connection. Phonse elaborated. "Nature, old man, people are gone mental on the nature. Geezers hiding behind a blind all day to get a picture of a bird! This is only a prototype. Once I build one with windows, so they can see all the little fishies . . . !" Phonse was satisfied that he had made his point.

"You said Uri had some kind of plan. I don't imagine the Bulgarians had the same recreational application in mind?"

"Russians, Dave, Uri was working for the Russian navy. He said these were going to be used to sneak into harbors and such, plant mines, take pictures, what have you."

"It seems strange that if Uri had this information, he wasn't more valuable to the government. If he was a submarine expert, surely our team would take an interest in —"

"Well, Dave, through the rigs and the jigs, I gathered that Uri couldn't afford to be too candid about his past, if you know what I mean." Phonse was conveying his meaning with a spastic series of winks and glances over his shoulder.

The R.S.V. certainly was a spectacular feat of engineering to have been undertaken in a facility as primitive as Phonse's shed. Its exterior was perfectly smooth, not a seam showed. Much like the navy submarines Dave had seen in St. John's harbor, it had an extension perpendicular to the main body, with little fins on the side. Dave supposed there must be a periscope in there somewhere.

"It's built for two men, Dave, old buddy, if you're interested in joining me on the first sea trial."

Though it looked convincingly like a submarine, Dave didn't believe for a second that the R.S.V. was actually functional. There was no way, especially considering Phonse's worries about being "crushed like a peanut," that he would ever go beneath the frigid North Atlantic in the R.S.V. "I don't think so, Phonse. I get seasick."

"I never thought of that, Dave. I wonder, do you get seasick in a submarine?"

"Claustrophobic too. I just couldn't do it, Phonse." Dave wasn't, or hadn't to that moment been, claustrophobic, but somehow the mere mention of the term caused him to feel confined in the big shed.

"Very well," said Phonse. Dave was glad Phonse didn't push it. "Though I may have to call on your assistance during the launch. The operation will have to be mounted under cover of darkness." When discussing matters technical, anything to do with the complex workings of machines, Phonse adopted a lofty tone that was at odds with his thick accent.

To extricate himself from what would surely be a marine misadventure resulting in Phonse's death, Dave figured it would be a good time to announce his intentions.

"I don't know, Phonse. I'm afraid I may not be here to help you."

"Why? What's up?"

"Phonse," Dave drew a deep breath, "I'm going to sell the Auk."

Phonse stared at Dave for a moment, then turned away shaking his head.

"It's not working out, Phonse. People aren't coming. I'm going bust."

Phonse sat on a sawhorse and took a long drink. He looked skyward and sighed.

"If I had any choice, Phonse . . . If there was anything at all . . ." This was breaking Dave's heart.

"Dave, though I've got to say that you are one of the best cooks I've ever met, I feel I must observe that there have been serious shortcomings in the marketing department over at the Auk."

"Perhaps that's it. Maybe it's just too isolated."

Phonse shook his head. "Nonsense. It's the marketing, old man, poor marketing. Isolation's got nothing to do with it. That should be part of the appeal. Going to a restaurant like the Auk, with the wine and everything, it's a special-occasion thing. People would drive out. Christ, old man, you've got geezers flying up here from all over the world to get a good gawk at a whale or take a snap of a gannet. People would —"

Phonse stopped. His eyes narrowed and a smile crossed his face. He jumped up from the sawhorse, turned a wobbly pirouette, grabbed the bottle of rum and filled Dave's glass. Dave was getting drunk.

"Dave, my friend, I have —" Phonse stopped again. "First, take another snort of that cocaine."

Dave was puzzled.

"Go on. Go on, b'y." Phonse gestured toward the pile of powder on top of the barrel. Dave complied.

"It's so clear, Dave. Now promise me you'll give it a second chance."

Dave wasn't sure.

"Listen! Just do this one thing for me. I mean, if you want to sell the Auk, you would be in a much better negotiating position to be pitching a going concern. Christ, Dave, they'll fleece you for an empty restaurant."

Dave had already considered the problems he faced selling a failed enterprise and nodded. Phonse took the gesture as an acceptance of his proposition.

"Here's the plan. We go to the library and get out some books on birds. We pick one that's really rare. You with me?"

Dave wasn't but nodded anyway.

"You call that birdy show on the CBC Radio and tell them you're after spotting this rare creature out here by the restaurant!"

Dave had definitely consumed too much rum. Though he was familiar with the radio program, the plan wasn't making any sense. Confused, he shook his head.

"Dave!" Phonse was now dancing a little jig, hopping foot to foot with the rum bottle in one hand, his glass in the other. "The crowd of bird-watchers will be all over the place, they'll be tromping around all day looking for the thing, the sun will go down, they'll be half starved . . ." Phonse stopped, looking at the cocaine on the barrel. "How often do you have to snort that stuff to keep a buzz on?"

Dave didn't say anything. He obediently inhaled another line. To do otherwise would have been rude.

Phonse continued. "The food you serve will blow their birdy minds! *Wait!* No duck on the menu, Dave, no birds at all, could be a sensitive point. I'm telling you, Dave, this is an excellent, A-1, top-drawer, money-making scheme."

It might be a deceit but the plan had its merits. Dave put his face to the barrel to suck up another line. No! It was truly ingenious. They would never be exposed and Dave could easily sell a restaurant that was full of customers every night.

"Not Roe's crested waxwing, Dave! Something much more remarkable. You'll have bird-watchers from all over the world flying in here, my man, and they will spread the word of the fine cuisine to be had at the Auk." Phonse indicated a toast. Dave raised his glass.

"To Roe's crested waxwing, Phonse! To the call of the Auk." Dave began squawking and cawing like a demented bird. Phonse joined in. They raised their heads whistling, tweeting and zreeting like madmen, like fools, until they bent over with laughter like two dizzy young boys.

When Dave finally emerged from the shed, it was daylight. The forecast storm had come and gone in the night. Dave and Phonse had been rum cozy around the chubby wood stove as the outbuilding's timbers moaned against the gale. In the storm's wake, a clump of warm air rushed in over the land. The temperature had risen considerably since dinner and a tremendous mist was coming off the disappearing snow. Fog was also pouring off the bay. The entire landscape seemed to be showing through a thin coat of whitewash. A brilliant sun was up there somewhere, charging every drifting water particle, so that the air around Dave seemed to pulse. Springtime in Newfoundland. The warming air was causing glitter to fall from the trees, littering the crust of snow with ice. It looked like someone had broken thousands of wine glasses in the woods, the aftermath of a fairy wedding. Dave hadn't walked more than twenty paces and yet when he turned to look back at Phonse's house and the big shed, they had already disappeared into the gauzy white.

5

Alice straddled him, her back arched as she ground her hips against his. Her hands, clasped around his biceps, squeezed harder with each thrust. She brought her mouth to his, filling it with her tongue as he came. The slippery warm fluid gushed over his belly, up to his ribs, waking him, leaving him briefly confused, then disappointed, and finally embarrassed.

Dave had not experienced a wet dream in years. He muttered oaths as he staggered the throbbing miles from his bed to the bathroom. The light slapped at him, an interrogation, the tungsten filament flailing in its gigantic, resonant glass dome, translating every volt into torturous mockery. His head was pounding, the skull likely filled to bursting with vomit. In the mirror he noted two flaky trails of dried blood leading from his nostrils to his upper lip, giving him a rusty little Hitler mustache. His eyes, all frayed red strands and yellow spots, sat deep in puffy purple nests. Dave looked like he had taken a good beating.

He wiped himself, little specks of tissue adhering to the come that was clotting amidst the hair on his belly. A gurgling burp tasted of rum. He threw up in the toilet.

Dave switched from oaths to pleas for mercy.

It was time again to take the pledge, to swear off the bottle and powders and fumes forever. "Absolutely forever, God," was promised. The light from the bathroom provided enough illumination for Dave to make out a plastic bag of cocaine sitting on the night table. Phonse had given it to him as a sample he might show a prospective buyer. Like who? A shady underworld figure that frequented the late-night gatherings of his fellow sophisticates? What impression, in his booze-and-blow-induced flights of jabber, had he left with Phonse? Dave had been in Fisheries, not the Rolling Stones! It came back to him. He had mentioned Larry, a Keith to his Mick. He choked back another pulse of puke and grabbed the bag in terror.

Naked, dissolute, certain of apprehension, he raced to the wine cellar, twice smashing the same toe against two different door frames, bringing booze-thinned blood to the cuticle. His pleas for mercy grew more urgent and by the time he had hidden the bag of drugs in a case of 1990 Ducru-Beaucaillou and slumped on the cold stone floor, it was all he could do to stop from weeping. It was little wonder he didn't attempt a dash to the answering machine when he heard Claire's voice in the distance asking where he was.

In the restaurant's kitchen, Dave had to twice interrupt the preparation of his hangover tonic to steady himself against the counter lest he throw up on the spot. He was trying hard to keep down the three 222s he had consumed in a futile attempt to arrest the shit-kicking his head was taking. Dave had seen his father employ "the bread soda" against the violently churning gut — a tablespoon of baking soda in a glass of warm tap water — and it usually worked.

This morning, though, Dave was combating one of the very worst of hangovers, the suicide model, a quick death being preferential to the misery. The bread soda was merely a stopgap; he needed to lose the entire day in television, ginger ale, codeine and a gentle soup. End it early at nine p.m. with a cold beer and a real sleep.

He needed something to eat, but when he opened the fridge, the first thing he noticed were the eggs sitting in their little cradles. The thought, the notion, the sound of the word, "hey-eeeggh," made him ill.

He had definitely made his Jekyll and Hyde transformation from Dave to Fuck-Up Man again last night. And hadn't he made a deal with Phonse to call the CBC and announce the presence of some exotic bird in the vicinity of the Auk? Still, even now, in his condition, when the very sun itself seemed like a cancer, the idea was a good one. Yes, he would do the evil deed to get a better price for the restaurant.

When he came upstairs from the apartment, he noticed the light flashing on his answering machine, but didn't bother to play back Claire's message. Was it really his intention to work things out between them?

It seemed the temperature outside was still climbing. Clumps of wet snow were sliding noisily off the roof. The mist and fog had grown thicker. He could not see the water of Push Cove from the kitchen window. The steep hill out the back faded into a moist white wall of oblivion.

He should have returned to the apartment and his bed, but instead slipped on a pair of rubber knee boots and stepped outside. The wet air felt good, seeming thick enough to keep him suspended, buoyant. Sound and light were dampened to a tolerable level for Dave's tender head.

He closed his eyes and could feel the fog moving around him. Water beaded on his face and ran down his cheeks as if he was crying.

It must have looked bad, being found curled up asleep on the dining-room floor. Dave assured Phonse he had just lain down for a second, but sensed that he must have been asleep for a couple of hours. When he stood up, he felt infinitely better than when he first awoke that morning.

"Jesus, Phonse, I feel . . . great." However unlikely, it was true.

"Well, I wasn't top-drawer this morning, I can tell you, Dave."

"Guess not."

"Are we off, then?"

"What?"

"To the library, Dave, to find the right bird for our little plan."

"I know we agreed to it, Phonse, but . . ."

"Fail-safe Dave, the plan's fail-safe. I've even considered a few extra measures that will insure we don't get caught."

Getting caught hadn't even occurred to Dave. What would be the charge? The false reporting of a bird sighting?

"It's harmless enough anyway, so what if they don't see the bird, you know they'll spot others. There are birds enough for all around here. Sure there's owls and turrs and crows and sparrows. Any bird you would want."

"We have to be careful, Phonse. These people take it seriously, especially if we say it's something rare."

Phonse shook his head. "You don't come out and say you're after spotting a dodo bird, old man. You call in and say you don't know much about birds, but that you saw a strange one the other day. You describe it to them and then they'll be the ones to identify it. You're not on the hook for anything, you never make any false claim at all."

Phonse had it well rationalized.

"Come on, Dave, let's get to it."

"Does it have to be today, Phonse?" Dave needed more time to worry about it.

"The show comes on the radio tomorrow morning, Dave."

They agreed to take the Skoda.

Driving through the fog was an effort. Even with his face pressed against the windshield, Dave could only see just beyond the hood and had to use the narrow highway's faded dividing line as a guide. The locals exhibited considerably more confidence behind the wheel. Dave was passed twice. He winced at oncoming vehicles traveling at their usual breakneck speed. Dave thought that the drivers must have some inherited ability to see through the soupy stuff; natural selection was at work, those not carrying the gene responsible for fog vision were quickly culled from the treacherous roadways. Or it might be simpler. The whole crowd out here might just be nuts.

Phonse too was unconcerned, paying no attention to the road. "Dave," he said, "I couldn't help but notice last night . . ."

"Yes?" Phonse was going to suggest that he was a prime candidate for drug addiction and might want to seek counseling. Claire, monitoring Dave's boozing, had once said so.

"You were . . . how can I say it . . . affected! Yes, affected by Alice."

Dave, remembering his salacious dream, felt his neck reddening. "In what way, Phonse?"

"Those women, they can . . ." Phonse seemed ill at ease. "They have a powerful effect on men. It was the same with Debbie. I'm not really the marrying type, but I was at this tavern in Gull Tickle when I met her and two weeks later, I was hitched. Now what happened in those two weeks, I really don't recall, outside of . . . well, you know."

"Phonse, I'm . . . married." Dave just couldn't say "happily married."

"The girls' mother was a strange one, too. She could put away warts and thinking on her could stop a nosebleed. Scary, Dave. And the men out there, in Gull Tickle, they're . . . I don't know, they're like zombies."

Dave thought that yes, Alice, with those green eyes, could easily have turned him into her zombie.

"Not to worry, Phonse," said Dave, worried.

"Thought I'd give you fair warning."

"If this plan works, I won't be around that much longer anyway, Phonse."

"That's too bad, Dave. I'll miss you, I will."

Dave was touched.

"Now, tomorrow when you make the call," said Phonse, putting the brief intimacy behind them, "don't do it from the restaurant."

"Why not?"

"Just in case, Dave. If something goes wrong, we want to have our backs covered. I suspect they probably have some kind of call-tracing mechanism down there at the CBC."

"Do you think?" Dave asked, growing a little alarmed.

"Absolutely, in the event some lunatic calls in and says he's planning on skull-fucking the premier, what have you."

That he was conspiring with a man who blithely used the term "skull-fucking" did little to reassure Dave.

Phonse's elaborate planning — playing dumb for the bird expert on the radio and the surreptitious measures to avoid being linked to the call — gave the enterprise a criminal character. They would likely next be coming up with an alibi. Dave felt uncomfortable going into the library. What if someone would later remember having seen two suspicious characters sneaking around ornithology?

"And are those men in the courtroom now?"

"Yes, it's those two men right there, Your Honor."

Dave was also concerned that he might encounter someone he knew at the library. What would he say if they asked what had brought him there? "Oh, you know, continuing work on my latest monograph, *Brillat-Savarin and the Puff Pastry.*"

Phonse feared nothing. He walked boldly to a computer terminal and keyed in "birds." Dave had mistakenly assumed that he might have to show Phonse the way around the facility, but then this was a man who had fashioned a submarine in his shed.

Everyone in the library seemed so young, thought Dave. Hadn't he been an eager student just a couple of years ago? No, he had last attended a university nineteen years earlier. And to what end? So that he could now undertake mischief designed to trick a bunch of earnest bird-watchers into eating at his restaurant.

Somewhere in the building there was a shelf holding a copy of Dave's master's thesis, "Changes in Newfoundland Settlement Patterns After Confederation: Resettlement by Default." He knew it was never read.

The students were so lithe, so sexy. The building was full of athletic, handsome young men and women so tautly muscled they virtually bounced. It was a highly charged environment, crackling with sex. Dave's older brother, Lloyd (mad as a hatter, Lloyd would certainly have been institutionalized if he hadn't found a job in the fantasy land of Canadian television), once said that libraries were the sexiest of places, all silence and lewd daydreams. Lloyd insisted that half the people in any library were hiding a hard-on or damp panties. It was strange that so much of Lloyd's nonsense became, after careful scrutiny, astute observation. Time was proving Lloyd sane. And if Lloyd was sane, then what was Dave?

Phonse scratched something on a slip of paper and gestured for Dave to follow him.

Luckily there were no students in QL 671–699. Dave understood that students no longer studied *real* things. That aspect of scholarship was over and done with. These days they studied previous studies. A student in the bird field would, today, be off in a section of the library with new books, books dedicated to the discussion and reinterpretation of the old books that were now of interest to Dave and Phonse. It was no longer the meaning of all the words written about birds that mattered, but the words themselves, their discredited Homo sapien bias, their tyrannical anthropomorphic tendencies. Scholars the world over no longer got their piss hot over empirical evidence, but over the reasons it had been recorded in the first place. This was either a brilliant stroke by the academics, producing ever more material to be scrutinized and reassessed, or a fatal miscalculation — dissecting each dissection over and over again until there was nothing left worth looking at, just a bunch of endlessly worked-over frog guts.

Phonse was pulling volume after volume from the shelves, gleefully filling his arms with books on birds, almost teetering under their weight. Dave kept glancing over his shoulder, anxiously watching for a familiar face. Who? His peers were all so exhausted, they were beyond learning. Satisfied they had gathered enough material, Phonse indicated, with a flick of his head, that Dave should follow him to a quiet, secluded corner table. There he divided the books so that they each had a stack of equal height to scrutinize.

Dave thought Phonse could have been more discriminating. The first book he opened was dedicated to the preservation of rare species in New Zealand. Among the other books on the table in front of him were: a volume obviously written for children, a scholarly analysis of lark migration patterns and several field guides for bird-watching in England. Dave was attracted to a dusty old beast of a book. Its arthritic binding creaked with age as he opened it. Dave recognized the name on the frontispiece, Audubon, as being crucial to the birders' world. He began flipping, at first indifferently, through the color plates.

The pictures had a dark magic about them, the lurid paintings eerily still with hawks, ducks, grebes and snipes stuck in time, like stuffed specimens on some shelf, musty, redolent of formaldehyde. This was the effect despite the painter's evident attempt to give the figures life by capturing them in movement, taking flight, tearing at carrion with blood-stained bills, swirling around clumps of swollen ripe fruit, paddling dreamily about a bed of reeds. But the eyes of the birds had frozen the pictures, they were always so vacant that they robbed the depictions of all vitality. And Dave realized that this wasn't a shortcoming in the illustrator's technique; it reflected the genuine attitude of birds, never studying the world, never coming to conclusions, but simply witnessing and accepting. It was why they were so perfect, so dumb, and cruel.

Dave knew they were venturing into uncharted territory. The bird-watching business had a long history, and they were playing games with a near-religious obsession. Falsely claiming to spot a rare bird was heresy. True, there was probably little legal recourse if they were caught. But what vigilante action might be taken by the scandalized birders, the followers of the raven and the vulture?

Phonse came and sat alongside Dave, holding open several books. "Dave, I think I've found what we're looking for." Phonse showed him a picture of a wildly colored, ridiculous-looking creature — Campbell's dodger bird. Its pink-and-orange tail was unfurled like that of a peacock. Its head was bald but for two tufts of gray feathers above its eyes. The illustration showed it next to a fat breadfruit, positioned there either to indicate its diet, its habitat or its massive size. Dave read that it was a native of the islands of Vanuatu.

"Phonse, what would a bird like that be doing in Newfoundland? It's from the South Pacific."

"Blown off course, tropical storm during its annual migration from the steamy land of the coconut! What difference, that's not the issue, if you read on you will note that it is *extremely* rare."

"Phonse, if the claim is too wacky no one will take it seriously."

Phonse put a finger to his mouth to shush Dave. He spoke in a whisper. "You're probably right, Dave, but I think the bird should also have a certain amount of . . . you know . . ." Phonse put his hands to his chest, cupping them as if cradling two large breasts. "Sex appeal. Just look at this baby, the pink tail, the eyebrows. Now that, Dave, that is a bird to be watched!"

Dave had taken false comfort in Phonse's familiarity with the library. He could only imagine what liberties

Phonse must have taken with the finer points of submarine engineering and design.

"Granted, more people might show up to see a particularly spectacular specimen, but let's at least pick one that has Newfoundland as part of its range."

Phonse nodded in response, reluctantly accepting Dave's logic, and diligently went back to the books.

They had been in the library for three hours. Dave returned to the stacks and gathered up a collection of books on birds of the North Atlantic region. The books shared one element: they all contained some kind of elegy to the great auk. Some authors were firm and certain in their condemnation of Newfoundlanders in the case of the bird's extinction, telling of blood-thirsty boatloads heading out to the Funk Islands and pummeling the utterly helpless, flightless birds all the way to oblivion. Newfoundlanders, it was said, had a propensity for bashing things. Once through with the great auk, they moved on to baby seals. Guns and disease were the weapons of choice for the stupid Newfs' undeclared, somnambulatory campaign to rid the Island of its native Beothuk Indians.

Other scribes were more willing to spread the blame, implicating Spaniards, Portuguese, French and Faeroese — the lot of them coveting feathers and down, black-gummed, sea-weary and desperate for a taste of meat and eggs. All the writers and scientists seemed horribly, horribly melancholy about the auk. The great bird, present only in illustration, never having made it to photography, was an endearing thing, standing tall in formal black and white, with a crushing bill, striped for pride. Content in the fog; comfortable, almost sleepy, bobbing atop a half-frozen sea. The great auk was too generous, too full of trust, too peaceful to have shared centuries with men.

Dave felt like crying. That he had named his restaurant after the extinct creature wasn't in such bad taste. He resolved that it would be a homage.

Phonse again came around the table and sat next to him. He was clutching a book close to his chest, looking like a schoolgirl.

"Am I to presume, Phonse, that you have another candidate?"

"Oh, Dave, this is *the* bird." Phonse laid out the book on the table. The illustration showed not a bird but the hallucination of a bird. It was clearly a duck of some sort with a swept-back tuft of snowy-white feathers atop its head. The body of the bird looked like it had been colored by a disturbed child, with mad blotches of red and blue and a streak of mustard yellow. Dave was certain it had to be from the tropics. Phonse read from the text on the facing page.

"'Tasker's Sulphureous Duck — *Aythya flagitius*. Range: the Carolinas to the coastal waters off Newfoundland. Distinct from the Common Sulphureous by its unusual spotted markings and white head tuft. Now extremely rare. Last sighting by Dr. Hans Speidel, near Fox Bite, Newfoundland, March 1985.' It's spot on, Dave! Look here! It's a diver! It hangs out on the salt water! You just tell them you saw it on the bay by the restaurant and we are in business."

Dave had begun to doubt whether they would find an appropriate bird, had assumed that he would have an excuse for bowing out of the hoax. But this duck met all the criteria they had agreed upon. And Phonse had done so much work.

Phonse could barely contain his glee as they drove home. "You just watch, Dave! They'll be tromping all over the place, the place will be maggoty with bird-watchers." The purpose of the exercise was now irrelevant to Phonse, the caper itself was enough.

But Dave had grown too old, far older than his years really, to take adolescent pleasure in anything. There were no thrills any more, only doubts and concern. From where had this malaise come? Perhaps it was his mother's early death, watching her suffer and fade, cancer nibbling at her lungs like an hors d'oeuvre, making a main course of her liver and brain, and all the while saying that things would get better, that there were people in much worse circumstances, that you had to accept the things that you could not change. Dave accepted these things but worried about them nonetheless.

"You know what will happen, too?" Phonse continued. "One will catch a gull or a kittiwake out the corner of his eye and say, 'Did you see that?' and another one will say 'Yeah! I saw something!' and they'll go wild for it. Psychology of the mob, Dave, mass hysteria!"

Dave wondered if a mob and mass hysteria were really what they were after.

Dave grabbed a beer from the restaurant's fridge and headed straight for the apartment and his bed. A somber night in front of the tube was in order. He was grazing over the channels with the remote control when he spotted Claire. She was on the national news, chiming in from DC. Her hair was now pulled back so tightly that it seemed to tug at her face. The dress was cool blue and severe. She was thinner, bony.

"Liberals are overstating the case. Those in the media, or with an influence over those institutions, are confined to the urban centers and they're tripping over the homeless every day. Realistically, it's not a problem for most Americans."

Jesus, he hadn't returned her calls. They were still married, after all. Despite the state of their union, he owed her some courtesy. He muted the TV. No sense getting worked into a rage from listening to her dismiss the homeless. Dave thought he might be among their number soon enough. Would she one day find him asleep over an air duct and step over his filthy body in disgust? He picked up the telephone and dialed.

What if a man answered? Would he be hurt? Perhaps relieved? He got her machine.

"Hi, honey." It sounded forced, Dave thought. "This is no way to talk, is it?" Wrong again, suggesting that their long-distance relationship was untenable. "I saw you on television again. Nice dress, the blue one. I'll try again later. Had a wonderful meal over at Alphonse Murphy's the other night." He was running out of things to say. "Love you." It didn't seem true.

He hung up and returned to the television, switching to a Batman rerun. Sinister forces were headquartered in the sewers beneath Gotham. But Fuck-Up Man fell asleep.

6

Phonse's shouts awoke Dave. The alarm clock said 6:18. Dave rolled from the bed and padded off for the restaurant's kitchen.

"I went ahead and made some coffee, Dave." Phonse was taking liberties. He handed Dave a cup of his brew.

"What's the plan, Phonse?" Dave figured that if they were going to go through with the stunt, he might as well give himself over completely to the madman's control.

Phonse happily accepted command. "There's a pay phone outside the gas station at the beginning of the Lower Road, but you can hear the traffic, that might be suspicious. A better bet would be the one down by the soccer pitch. Nobody will be around and it's quiet."

Dave nodded. A poor soldier not fully understanding his mission, he was perfect cannon fodder.

"I've written down a description of the bird for you." Phonse handed him an index card with a careful listing of the bird's significant anatomical features and its behavior.

"Right, Phonse, but what's it called again?"

"Perfect, you don't need to know. Remember, you want *them* to decide what kind of bird it is. The less you know, the better."

It had come to that.

"Now, when you're talking, you'll want to disguise your voice a little. I suggest you hold your nose." Phonse pinched his nostrils. Dave just kept nodding. The plan was ridiculous.

"You coming with me, Phonse?"

"Oh no, I'll be monitoring the situation. You place the call at eight-fifteen. Not too close to the beginning of the show, but leaving enough time for them to figure out what you're talking about while they're still on the air."

"It's not going to work, Phonse."

"Dave, old man! Not to worry. Like a charm, it will."

Dave was checking his watch as he climbed into his car. Any kind of schedule made him tense. When he was a day jobber with Fisheries, he always woke early in anticipation of the alarm. Not a good man in the clutch. The cup of coffee Phonse had given him was working on his insides, churning up some of the residual rum, and Dave felt the need to use the toilet. It would have to wait.

As he headed up the drive he caught Phonse in his rearview mirror. The nutty geezer was grinning. Was he laughing at Dave, another sucker from St. John's?

There was activity on the Upper Road. Though it was just eight o'clock in the morning, the car wreckers were already on the beer. This early drinking might be a cultural remnant from the fishery, Dave thought, when the better part of a day's work would have been completed by this hour. Then again maybe it was just the national alcoholism.

The beer drinkers noted his passage, turning from their business and watching the road. They kept close tabs on the traffic, always seeking more automotive prey. They were potential witnesses to Dave's crime. And they would remember Dave's Skoda. Like wolves closing in on a lame caribou, they could tell the car wasn't long for the road.

Dave turned on the radio. The bird show was just beginning. The host, Bill "Buster" Bartlett, was bubbly and stupid as always. Despite having hosted the call-in program for years, he seemed to have retained almost no knowledge of birds and so remained fresh and interested, even fascinated, every week. Today the co-host, Dr. Jack Tomlinson, one of three rotating experts, started by announcing the return of various migrants. Some had traveled as far as one thousand miles, he said. "Wow!" said Buster, as if he had never before heard this striking fact.

Dr. Jack had an English accent, as did the first two callers, good Brits suffering, futilely, to bring civilization to the colonies. These callers were clearly regulars, not posing questions, but announcing sightings with scientific authority. They would, no doubt, be among the dupes daring the cliffs around the restaurant in search of the curious and rare duck. Dave wondered whether he should affect an English accent when he called. Maybe not.

"A yellow cap, you say!" said Dr. Jack. "That would indicate a male black-backed three-toed woodpecker."

"I'm certain it was a hairy," the caller countered. "It had a white back. I'm sure of it."

"It's the yellow cap, caller, that puzzles me. There are rare aberrant immature hairys with the cap. That would be exciting."

"Now, Dr. Tomlinson," Buster cut in, "I've always wondered, what kind of woodpecker was Woody?"

"I'm sorry, Buster?"

"Woody Woodpecker, what species was he? I know, of course, that he was only a cartoon character, but what kind of bird was the character based on?"

"I'm really not sure, Buster," said Dr. Tomlinson.

The dirt parking lot of the soccer pitch had suffered badly from the ravages of winter. It was pocked with enormous, water-filled potholes. Phonse had selected the location wisely. It was two hundred feet off the main road and shielded from view by a small grove of dogberry trees. Dave would not be spotted making his call.

He stopped the car alongside the phone booth, which, besides the two soccer goals, was the only structure in sight. It was odd, the phone booth being out there. It certainly couldn't see much use. It was another of the many odd totems around Newfoundland, signs that someone had once imagined that something would be happening somewhere, and now no one could recall why. There were community wharfs built in towns that no longer had a fishery. There were soccer pitches and softball diamonds miles from any settlement. There were roads leading nowhere. Perhaps these projects were like the wooden planes built by the cargo cults, ghostly activity undertaken to attract somebody with a real purpose, industrial decoys.

It wouldn't work, thought Dave, nature was reclaiming Newfoundland in the name of the Beothuks and the great auk. The wharfs would wash away, the softball diamonds would become bogs and the phone booth would sink into the damp earth. Newfoundland resisted civilization. The ancient Dorset peoples had failed. The Point Revenge Indians had failed. The Norse had failed. The Basques had failed. And now the British Empire and its Canadian water boys were failing. The island belonged to the black bears and caribou and lynx and crows. And they would soon have it back.

Dave pulled the index card from his jacket pocket. Swept-back white tuft on the head, red and yellow body markings against a white background. Easy enough.

He placed the card on the dashboard and lit a cigarette. All the crooks in the movies did this, smoked in a car before knocking over some joint, before moving in for the kill.

A local voice came over the radio. A woman in Capahayden had spotted an unusual bird out her kitchen window. This was good, thought Dave, finally a query from a novice. Her husband had taken a shot at it but missed.

Dave stepped from the car and noticed the ground was littered with used condoms in silly Day-Glo oranges and purples. Perhaps young backseat lovers used the lonely phone booth all the time.

It was eight-fifteen.

He noticed his palms had grown sweaty. There was

more distress in his bowels.

"Thank you for calling *Avian Week*. Please hold."

There was still time to hang up.

"Hello, caller."

He had to hang up, if he said one word, it would be too late, he would have to go through with it. He would have finally descended to Phonse's level of reasoning, abandoning all those years in polite society to join a gang of bay outlaws.

"Do we have a caller on the line?"

"Yes, hello, am I on the air?" It was what they all said.

"Hello, caller, this is Jack Tomlinson." They were helping him along.

Dave couldn't remember whether he had disguised his voice or not when he first spoke. Now he spoke through his nose.

"I'm after seeing the strangest bird."

"Could you describe it for us, please."

"Well it was, it had . . ." Dave's heart was racing. He should never have sucked back that coffee.

"Are you listening to your radio, caller? Please turn down your radio," said Buster.

"It was like a duck, right. But it had a white tuft on its head and it was red and yellow."

"Red and yellow?" Dr. Tomlinson didn't believe Dave for a second.

"No. It was white with red and yellow markings."

"Where did you see this bird, caller?"

"In Push Cove. Out by Push Through."

"Ah," said Tomlinson, "on the salt water, that's

different. Near that restaurant, is it? My students took me there once. Lovely spot, although the name of the place escapes me."

"Yeah, that's right. Out by that restaurant." Dave had the urgent need to shit. His guts were boiling. Why hadn't he gone before leaving the restaurant?

"How many of these ducks did you see?"

"Just the one, it had a tuft on its head."

"That's curious. Did you see it diving under water for long periods of time? I'm just trying to get an indication of its behavior. It doesn't sound familiar."

Did it dive? Dave dug in his pocket for the crib sheet. He had left it in the car.

"Please turn down your radio, caller, you're listening to the delay." Buster was losing his patience.

Did it dive? "I didn't see it dive. It was far away."

"Well," said Tomlinson, "it doesn't sound like anything I've ever seen."

"Right, okay," said Dave.

"Sorry we can't help you, caller," said Buster and it was over.

Dave hung up, having failed yet again. He dashed to the car. His hands were trembling and he was concerned he would shit in his pants.

He started the engine and put the Skoda in reverse. From out of nowhere he heard angry, high-pitched screams, saw flashes of color through the window on the passenger side.

He had been so focused on the phone call and getting himself to a toilet that he had not noticed the arrival of three young girls on bicycles. One of the girls had narrowly escaped being run over. What were they doing riding bicycles at this time of the year? Where did they imagine they were living? What were they doing at the soccer pitch?

The girls, snot-nosed ragamuffins, were looking right at him. They would remember his face. One girl, she couldn't have been more than ten years old, came toward the driver's window. She had either raspberry jam or a sore at the corner of her mouth.

"Mister, you almost killed me. Get your head out of your ass!"

"Are you fucking nuts, or what?" said another of the girls.

Dave put the car in drive and stepped hard on the accelerator. Get out fast before they get the license number, he thought. He pulled hard on the steering wheel, trying to spin the car around. The back wheels slid across the wet mud of the parking lot, the front of the car was adrift. With a jolt that snapped Dave's neck sideways, the rear right fender crashed into the phone booth, setting loose a pom-pom of blue sparks from the wires above.

"He's fucking crazy."

"You mental, buddy?"

The collision steadied the car, which now pointed straight toward the lane leading to the main road. Dave stomped on the gas again, the car lurched forward, found some solid gravel and sped away. In the rearview mirror he saw the girls passively examining the overturned phone booth.

When he hit the highway, a voice came through the pounding in his ears. He had left the radio on. It was Phonse.

"I saw that bird too. Twice I saw it. Incredible sight. Very colorful creature. Once it was way off on the water and it dived for the longest time, came to the surface a good distance from where it went down. Second time though was really strange, it was walking, you know in a sort of wobbly way, on the beach. Never seen the like."

"On the beach?" Tomlinson was riveted.

"Yes, strange, what?"

"My God!"

"What is it, Jack?" Buster was fascinated.

"Well, I can only suggest that Hans Speidel has finally been vindicated. We have two listeners describing what could only be Tasker's sulphureous duck."

Yes! thought Dave. Phonse had fooled the fuckers! Two callers! A brilliant stroke by the old dear.

Buster asked, "Why does this vindicate Hans Speidel, Jack?"

"It was thought extinct until a sighting in . . . Fermeuse, or Fox Bite I think it was, by the noted ornithologist Hans Speidel. Most experts felt Speidel must have been mistaken. Now, caller, I would also like to know —"

"Wait, Jack, it seems we've lost him."

Thought extinct! They were looking for rare, not extinct. Phonse had given them the auk. The Eskimo curlew had seemed a reasonable bet, there were perhaps only ten of those left, but they were found on northern barrens. Phonse hadn't saved the day, he had ensured that their harmless subterfuge would be subjected to serious scrutiny. There was another caller on the line.

"Dr. Tomlinson, where did they say they spotted that Tasker's sulphureous?"

7

As he overshot the driveway leading to Phonse's, Dave realized that he had, in his panic, been speeding all the way from the soccer pitch. The tires of the Skoda screeched as he pulled it hard around from the pavement and on to the gravel path to Phonse's place. The timid vehicle was shaking, never having known such excitement.

He pulled up in front of the shed, expecting Phonse inside. But Phonse emerged from the bushes over near the restaurant. Dave ran to him.

"Phonse, we've got to hide the car, Jesus, if those girls talk . . . they will too! The police will be asking about the phone booth. Or worse, the phone company. We'll put the car in the shed."

"Dave! Calm down, man!"

"I knocked over the phone booth, with the car, there were sparks and there were these girls on bikes!"

"DAVE!"

Dave realized his shirt was heavy with sweat and growing cold against his flesh.

Phonse spoke quietly and carefully to settle him. "You knocked the phone booth over with the car?"

"Yes, Phonse. I panicked, I guess."

"I know."

"What? How?"

"I could tell from your voice on the radio. All the deep breathing. I'm sure they were worried you were going to start barking obscenities over the air any second." Phonse laughed at this.

"Oh, God."

"It was perfect, Dave. In the end you came off like a proper simpleton."

"Why is that good, Phonse?"

"They would never suspect any scheme from such an arsehole. Now, you say some girls saw you knock over the phone booth?"

"Yeah, I was trying to get out of there before they got my license plate and the car skidded into the phone booth. I'm sure they'll talk."

"Young girls?"

"Yes."

"Not to worry, they'll never say a word."

"Why not?"

"Because everyone would immediately assume they had something to do with it. They know they'd be blamed and they'll keep their mouths shut. Even if they did say anything, you would just deny it. What would you be doing using the phone up at the soccer pitch?"

"Calling the radio."

"Dave, Columbo works in Los Angeles, which is on television. Calm yourself, get over to the restaurant and start peeling spuds. The place is going to be alive with bird brains this afternoon."

Phonse was right. It wasn't as though they had pulled a bank job. Dave felt better.

"Were you planning on calling all along, Phonse?"

"Always have a Plan B, Dave, always have a contingency." Phonse grinned. "What you don't know, Dave, or what you cannot seem to accept, is that you really never know what's going to happen next."

Was this true, was that the logic governing this caper — happenstance, chaos? Dave couldn't pursue the matter. His bowels called.

"Phonse, I've got to shit something awful."

"Two kinds of people in the world, Dave, those whose arseholes seize up in a crisis, and those who shit themselves. Go on into the house." Phonse waved Dave on and strolled to his shed, shaking his head.

The matter was urgent enough that Dave should have run to the toilet, but his dignity kept him to a quick, businesslike trot.

Once in the front door, Dave realized he didn't know the location of the bathroom. Drinking two nights earlier, Dave and Phonse had relieved themselves in the snow just outside the shed's big barn doors.

"Hello?"

There was no response, though it felt to Dave there was someone about. The house smelled of baking bread. He headed up the narrow stairs.

"Hello?"

The bathroom was at the top of the stairs. Dave hurriedly entered and undid his pants.

Quite unlike the rest of the house, the bathroom was sterile, modern and suburban. Understandably, there was little nostalgia for antique toilet facilities. It always struck Dave as odd that people who had Victorianized their old homes in St. John's carried the theme to the bathroom, filling an old piss pot with potpourri, lining the windowsills with old blue and green patent medicine bottles. You just knew these happy yuppies never had to crouch over a cold porcelain chamber pot at three o'clock in the morning, choking back a spoonful of castor oil to hasten the adventure.

Next to the toilet there was a magazine rack in which Dave was surprised to find an old issue of the *Times Literary Supplement*. Who read the *TLS*? Probably Alice. But then why not Debbie or Phonse? He had never shaken his St. John's bigotry, still equating a thick accent and overalls with some lack of sophistication. Surely the past days had shown him the fool. On top of the paper's fold was a review of a biography of one Nikola Tesla, who appeared to be some kind of inventor. Beneath the fold there was something concerning the Cathars.

Anxiety had wreaked havoc on his insides. Dave noted he was certainly among the "shit themselves" number. He supposed that Phonse's delineation separated the great men from the masses. He imagined Churchill, sphincter locked with bulldog determination, poring over maps as bombs rained upon London, while lesser men rushed to the shitters.

He stepped from the bathroom and came face to face with Alice.

"I thought I heard something. I was asleep," she said.

She did smell of sleep, woolly and warm. In contrast, Dave was quickly being engulfed by a disgraceful wall of stink. He closed the bathroom door. It was no remedy; the hallway remained foul and he was pinned by Alice, who, rubbing her eyes, seemed to be going nowhere.

"Are you looking for Phonse?" she said. "He's usually up and gone by now."

"Oh, no, I . . . just . . . back seeing Phonse." How nervous she made him, turning him into a schoolboy. "The other night, I left my watch."

His watch! Why would he have left his watch? Why didn't Alice move? Did she want him to kiss her, had she woken from a dream about Dave only to find her *objet de désir* in the hallway outside her bedroom. He should kiss her, he thought. He wanted to.

"Dave?"

"Yes?" And yes and yes.

"Can I get in the bathroom?"

"Oh, of course." He stepped aside. Alice went into the bathroom. She turned before closing the door.

"See you later."

Sipping a nerve-steadying Calvados in the kitchen at the Auk, Dave once again saw the end of the restaurant. The stunt with the radio show would make for a funny story in years to come. He would amuse his dining companions at various soup kitchens with the tale of his fall from grace. "I owned a restaurant once," he would begin.

But through the window he saw a human figure gingerly tiptoeing its way through the bushes. Squinting, Dave made out a large woman, in a floppy hat, heavily laden with scopes and binoculars and one of the fearsome gunlike cameras that had given him such a start at Larry Doyle's. Surely it couldn't be a mark from the radio con — it was too soon.

The woman's neck was craned as she painstakingly scanned the treetops. She carefully picked single steps so as not to make a sound. Surely it couldn't be. Dave went for the door.

"Hello."

She was briefly startled by the man clasping the morning snifter. The optical gear tethered to her neck swung around like a sling as she turned to face him.

"Oh, hello." English accent! It figured. "You must be the restaurateur." The apple spirits gave him away.

"Can I help you, Madame?" Having been pegged as a restaurateur, Dave felt like playing the poncy cook with French affectations.

"I've just come about the bird."

No! Were people that easily had?

"Bird, Madame?"

"Then you haven't heard. There's been quite a remarkable sighting, down at your beach."

"I caution you it's not much of a beach, and no, I've heard nothing about this . . . bird." He said "bird" with scorn, French cooks thinking only of birds roasted and paddling through a Madeira sauce.

"Well then, I ..." The affected version of Dave seemed to be having its effect. The woman didn't know quite what to say. "If it's fine with you, I won't be any trouble. I've parked in your lot. I could move the car."

"The lot is for customers."

"Oh, I had no idea you were open. I thought ..."

Dave sniffed noisily, deriding her presumption.

"Perhaps lunch then, if you have a table. Actually, I've heard it's quite good."

"I am sure you will not be disappointed. What time?"

She consulted a heavy watch. "One?"

"Best of luck in your quest."

In an hour Dave had six tables booked and nothing to serve them. Not only was he unprepared, his glee over getting a chance to cook again was tempered by a touch of stage fright. He hadn't danced with his stove for some time. After searching the freezers he called Phonse.

"Can you do me a big, big favor?"

"You need supplies, don't you? You should have picked them up right after the phone call."

"I guess."

"You didn't think it would work, did you, Dave?"

"No."

"Give us a list."

Dave hadn't time to give a menu proper consideration and so listed every fresh provision he could think of: green lettuces, radicchio, scallions, red and yellow peppers, goat cheese, veal cutlets, mussels and oysters.

From the freezer he had retrieved a couple of pork tenderloins, three dozen lamb kidneys he'd been saving for himself and several tubs of frozen stock.

In the kitchen his mind was racing. He cut the thawing pork into medallions, placed appropriate measures of rice at the ready and plunged the kidneys into a big bowl of cool milk.

Wines! He returned from the cellar with a case of various bottles to replenish the stock behind the bar, lunch wines, youthful rosés and Beaujolais, a palate-cleansing Santenay, a brash California Zinfandel, two mellowing Riojas for the meat eaters and a trio of altogether too dear white Burgundies.

The Pommery mustard was missing. The garlic had sprouted. The olives were beginning to wrinkle. So Alice, delivering the groceries, found Dave wilting under the strain. She laid several bags on the floor and looked at him, seemingly disappointed.

"Come on, there's more in the truck," she said. Little boy Dave did as he was told.

Phonse had been wise to give Alice the task of fetching the supplies. She had thought to buy fresh garlic, and leeks, and Belgian endives, and salmon and halibut steaks, and noticing that he hadn't considered a dessert, some lovely ripe fruit.

Dave didn't have the time to thank her properly. If he wasn't busy making a mustard sauce for the kidneys (Alice had spotted the big earthenware jar of Pommery in clear view), he might have kissed her feet.

She also had the presumption to write the menu on the

chalkboard by the bar, even adding a salade niçoise. "It's lunch, Dave! Not dinner. People are not going to eat kidneys." When the first customers arrived, she stopped Dave from leaving for the dining room with a firm hand on his shoulder. "You're perspiring . . . heavily. Stay here."

She went to her shoulder bag, pulled out a clean blouse and changed in front of him. Dave tried resisting, tried to play at being disinterested, but could not help but glower at the curve of her hips, at the full brassiere, at her lips as she spread them with red.

Alice responded to his gaze."Do I look okay?"

"Alice. You look like about the best thing —"

"Good." She went for the tables. Through the door Dave could hear her greeting the hungry birders. "Good afternoon. For three? Any luck?"

She swung through the kitchen like a professional, giving orders — "Two niçoises, pork Calvados" — as she grabbed prepared plates and returned to tend her tables.

Birders apparently having met other birders, dragged them back to the Auk. Seven tables were full and from the sound of it, Dave judged they were having a splendid time.

"Finally, Dave, lamb kidneys, grilled halibut, and can you poach the salmon?"

Dave was back in stride, no request would be denied. "In champagne, I can." It was a new idea, a bold experiment.

"And the cellar? The salmon has asked for a Meursault-Charmes."

"I have half-bottles of the '88." Dave was suddenly serious. "Did the salmon have an appetizer?"

"The little goat cheese toasts with that tomato paste."

"Coulis. Coulis of sun-dried tomatoes." Alice made a face, cocking her head and preciously mouthing "coulis." Dave continued. "The cellar is down those stairs. Which table is the salmon?"

"Closest to the bar."

"The Meursault is in the furthest corner of the cellar, you can't miss the half-bottles."

Alice headed for the cellar. Dave went to the swinging door. Through one of the tiny diamond-shaped windows he studied the table nearest the bar. Two men and a woman. They were dressed in the mock fishing vests, cableknit sweaters and leather patches of the class that chose to go out of doors. You could tell they had never worked a day under the sky. They *took the air*. The woman, middle-aged, was slightly flushed from her rejuvenative exercise. She was smiling, at some bon mot, he guessed. She was elegant and at ease. The men had full heads of perfectly groomed hair, gone gracefully gray at the temples.

Alice returned.

"Look for a good tip, Alice. The Meurseult costs two hundred a half."

No piece of salmon had ever been so delicately poached. The bouillon of champagne, herbs and scallions massaged the fish, which was then dressed up for the opera in a butter jacket with caper buttons. The glistening pink flesh sat on a plate gilded with julienned vegetables that remained crisp and presentable in the heat. Dave wanted the table with the salmon to tell her deep-pocketed friends about her fah-bulous lunch at the Auk.

It wasn't right, but Dave had no choice but to keep the lamb kidneys on the evening menu; there simply wasn't anything else. Alice again had to race to St. John's immediately after lunch so that the nine tables for dinner could enjoy one of two soups: a crab bisque, wasp-stung with red chili and coriander, or caribou consommé with wild chanterelles. They could then move on to rabbit braised with red wine, duck magrets with a green peppercorn sauce (which proved popular despite Phonse's warning) or a rather pedestrian spinach and ricotta cannelloni. Dessert was limited to fresh fruit sorbets in a cold lime soup and a couple of berry pies.

As the last of the diners were sipping their coffees, slouching sleepily and contentedly in their chairs, Dave, following Alice's instructions, changed into fresh whites and wandered among the tables checking to see that everything had been to his customers' satisfaction. He heard whispers, "He's the cook," "Oh, that was just lovely." He heard romances rekindled by the wine, the food and the candlelight, "You look lovely," "What a wonderful day this was." He acknowledged the many compliments given him with liberal Armagnacs, on the house. Dave bathed in it. It was a happy room.

He overheard tables talking of birds. Though there had been no sulphureous duck, there had been many other birds: juncos, grosbeaks and siskins, in the woods, gulls, ospreys and bald eagles at the water. It had been a productive day, a grand day for birds. No one was disappointed they hadn't spotted the rare creature yet; it would take time, perhaps the duck was moving around the coast. But Dave, eavesdropping on the table to his back while pretending to listen to another, nodding in agreement with anything said, heard it declared that the area was truly a perfect site for the sulphureous and that it would surely return.

The last of the late seating were not gone until midnight. Dave sat at the bar considering whether he had enough energy to lift a drink to his mouth. Alice came and sat next to him.

"Alice, without you ..."

"It was nothing, Dave."

"You've obviously worked in a restaurant before."

"Yeah, in Montreal. The cook was almost as good as you."

Smiling at this flattery consumed Dave's last reserves of energy. Alice helped herself to the Armagnac. Dave noticed how carefully she tasted it, how she rolled her tongue around her mouth. Her fatigue showed. There was a rose flush high on her cheeks. Her shirt was wrinkled. Perspiration had made her short hair a little spiky.

"How much do I pay you, Alice, to come back tomorrow?" Just looking at Alice was drawing the frost of loneliness and regret out of his bones. He would have paid her anything.

"We'll work it out. I did well on the tips. Funny how careless Newfoundlanders are with money. They sense the end is nigh, I guess." She yawned. "Shit, I'm tired."

She flicked an ankle, letting one of her black loafers drop to the floor. She lifted the hard-worked foot into her lap and massaged the sole.

Dave could smell the warm hosiery. He wanted to take her foot in his hands. He wanted to bring her to bed, curl up against her, feel her sleep, wake her with a milky coffee, watch her in the tub. But he remained speechless, paralyzed.

"I need to go to bed, Dave. I'll come by tomorrow. I can't go back and forth to town for supplies, though. That was too much."

"No, I'll take care of all that."

"And you need at least one other waitress, properly two, to work that room when it's full."

"Yes, of course, Alice, absolutely."

"Do you want me to hire somebody?"

"Yes. Yes, I do."

Alice walked around the bar to the kitchen door. Then she stopped. She turned back to Dave.

"Where's your wife? Phonse said you were married."

He talked into his drink. "She's in Washington, DC. She lives there now."

Alice considered this for a moment and then left without saying good night.

8

Dave traveled to Push Through the next morning to once again contract Bet Boland as kitchen help. Short, softly round Bet, who washed dishes and prepared vegetables. Bet, who, after only cursory instruction, had become quite a good cook in her own right, was Bet and not Betty because, as her family informed Dave, she was retarded. Her reedy older sister, Doris, would look at "poor Bet," shake her head and say, "Retarded, retarded, retarded." While Bet was certainly not an intellectual giant, she scarcely deserved such a cruel assessment. Bet's biggest problem, Dave knew, was that her family was "insane, insane, insane." Without Bet, the Auk could never make it. Soon after the restaurant had first opened, Bet replaced both a drunken, surly dishwasher and a schizophrenic sous-chef (a vegetarian who, after turning a chlorophyll green, came to believe Dave was Satan).

Bet went upstairs to ready herself for work the moment Dave came in the door, as if no time had passed since her last engagement months earlier. Dave was left to chat with

Doris, who was chain-smoking as she operated a cigarette-rolling machine.

The lightning-fast rate of cigarette production barely matched consumption in the house. The middle air of the front room held a permanent band of chalky blue haze.

"Back at it again, are we then, Mr. Purcell?" Doris asked, a sloppy cigarette dangling from her lips.

"Yes, quite miraculously things have picked up again."

"Vince said it would never last, you know." Vince was Doris's husband and a lout of legend.

"Thank God he was wrong, hey?"

Doris stopped rolling and took an especially deep drag from her smoke, so loosely constructed that it just about burst into flames. Maybe she had hoped Vince was right. It was an odd tendency of Newfoundlanders to relish the failure of their neighbors and then offer a hand getting them back on their feet. At least failure ensured humility and a healthy fear of God's strange ways.

"Funny things going on in the woods up your way, Mr. Purcell." Doris squinted at Dave as if he was in some way involved.

"What do you mean, Doris?"

"People up there at night, snooping around." Doris paused and then whispered, "With equipment."

Equipment? It could only be the dreaded Winnebagos.

"What kind of equipment, Doris?"

"Funny cameras."

"Oh, they're bird-watchers."

"Bird-watchers! I'm not sure we want that kind of thing going on around here. What kind of birds are they watching, anyway? And why? How foolish, running around at night looking at birds. I know now they don't have the time to waste. Probably got the best kind of government jobs . . ."

Dave stopped listening. Doris was beginning a rant that would eventually include an indictment of the "the crowd from the university," "state terror" — by which she meant municipal taxes and regulations — and "the savages on the Upper Road." Her tirade concluded, as usual, with an attack on Alphonse Murphy. Just as Bet came down the stairs, Doris was saying, "That Alphonse Murphy, he's in with them. And that Romanian friend of his, Uri Svetkov, what do you suppose he was up to before he disappeared? I have nothing against foreigners now, Mr. Purcell, but this Uri fellow . . ." It was no wonder Bet was always so anxious to go to work.

Dave's preparation for lunch was frequently interrupted by the phone. He was soon booked solid for a week.

Alice breezed in at eleven o'clock and promptly went to work setting tables. There was no chance, especially with Bet cleaning the kitchen around him, to have any intimate conversation with her. She smiled at him in a friendly way as they crossed paths. Alice was kind, he thought. But was there any sign that she felt even the tiniest, fleeting, momentary desire for him? He scrutinized her every gesture, worked over every glance in his mind and learned nothing. Dave thought he must be an open book. Alice, with her mysterious power, her hypnotic eye, must have noticed the deep longing in his gaze, must have sensed that Dave was studying her every move with growing interest. Whenever Alice was in the same room Dave felt an intense heat building inside him.

The big hits at lunch were the penetrating garlic soup and the salad of dandelion greens, roasted onions and a smokey local bacon. The bread Bet baked that morning would not last through the night. The spring chill made for hungry lunchers.

Alice was bringing in the last plates when Dave finally made an effort to engage her.

"What's the word, Alice? Happy customers?"

"Very. Though no sightings of this rare bird." Alice didn't stop to talk, didn't look Dave in the eye. Dave wondered how much she knew of the scam.

"Amazing bit of luck for me, what?"

"Quite." Alice stopped stacking dirty dishes for Bet. Turning to Dave, she wiped her hands in a towel and walked to him, coming to stand very close. "It's a curious obsession, hey?"

Was she talking of birding or Dave's obvious lust? He almost forgot what they had been talking about and sputtered a response.

"Birding? Curious? I wouldn't have thought. Nature and all. Quite wonderful. They're beautiful, birds."

Alice smiled, looked away, suppressing a laugh. For no good reason Dave felt vaguely embarrassed.

"You don't think so?" he asked.

"Oh, no, yes, birds . . . very beautiful . . . But these people, these birders, some of them are very funny. Do you know about the twitchers?" She laughed out loud, her eyes lighting up, her teeth flashing.

"Twitchers?"

"There are apparently two schools of bird-watching, those that enjoy the, I don't know, the aesthetics of the birds and are happy to just look and admire them, and then there are the twitchers, who, once they've seen a species, check it off and move on. They're like collectors, I guess, obsessives. The lunch crowd seemed to think that you are soon going to be inundated with twitchers from all over the globe" — she laughed again — "and they don't like it."

She seemed to know nothing of the duck hoax, and he would never tell her. He reasoned that if Alice was to discover the horrible fraud he was perpetrating on these innocent, well-meaning bird lovers to simply fill his pockets and rescue his pride, she would think him cruel and selfish.

"Inundated. I like the sound of that."

"Yes, with twitchers and experts."

Experts? No, Dave didn't want any experts near the restaurant. Experts would sense something was wrong, would be wise to the canard. Experts would expose him.

Alice returned to the kitchen to help Bet. The two women seemed to be hitting it off fabulously.

By eight o'clock Dave was beginning to weaken. The restaurant had not been so busy since its inaugural night, and Dave had not accounted for the fatigue that would accompany success. He hadn't a moment to stop, no time to have a smoke and relish the succulent fruits of mischief. Bet was less affected by the rush. She never grew agitated or scrambled madly about the kitchen as Dave did. She possessed a native ability to budget her energy and always managed to keep a smile on her face. Alice too was a serious worker, focused and efficient, a professional waitress, charging, all shoulders and business, in and out of the kitchen but floating through the dining room.

As he was retrieving a case of wine from the cellar (there were calls for more Rioja), it occurred to Dave that the little pick-me-up he required was hidden in a case of Ducru-Beaucaillou in the corner. The plastic bag was much bigger than he remembered, full of enough cocaine to land Dave in jail. He knew he should flush it down the toilet, but helped himself to a line anyway. And another. He would flush it tomorrow. Once he got into the swing of things it would no longer be necessary.

Back upstairs Dave certainly felt more on top of things. The heat of the kitchen was not nearly as oppressive as it had been just minutes earlier, and although the food he was preparing looked less appetizing, cooking was fun. What was the public outrage, the foofaraw, about cocaine anyway? he wondered. The stuff wasn't so dangerous. It certainly helped him cope with the crush of orders Alice was delivering. But did Alice know something was amiss? He thought she might have shot him a disapproving look when she picked up the fusilli with wild mushrooms and the Mediterranean-style fish stew.

Just after ten o'clock Dave returned from the cellar again. The only problem with cocaine, he thought, was that its pleasant effects dissipated so quickly. Alice was waiting for him as he came up the stairs with yet another case of wine.

"I think we're okay on the wine, Dave."

"Probably right, Alice. What was I thinking?" She knows, he thought. Was there white powder ringing his nostril?

"You've got company."

"What?" Dave wondered whether he was being busted.

"Phonse is out there."

Dave set down the wine and rushed to the little windows in the kitchen door. Phonse was there looking like a mad trapper, sitting with some puzzled diners. He was evidently telling them some tale, extending his arms wide to indicate something of great size. The woman at the table appeared to be shocked. Dave went into the dining room, heading straight for the attentive guests.

"How are we enjoying dinner?" he asked coolly. The cocaine helped him think on his feet. He was a new and better man under this powder's spell. The woman looked up at him.

"Oh," she said (another British accent), "oh it's just scrumptious. The caribou consommé was —"

"I see you've met Alphonse Murphy."

The woman's dinner companion, a white-haired geezer wearing a cravat, jumped in.

"Yes, he's just been telling us the most extraordinary tale. Of finding dinosaur bones, fossils," he said.

Dave looked down and saw Phonse smiling up at him. It was a sinister smile, the smile of a child who had got away with some horrible devilment.

"Over on my property, Dave," said Phonse, "a Raptor of some sort, I would imagine. Jesus-big jawbone. Snap a man in half with one good chomp. I'll call the crowd at the university tomorrow so they can come up and have a look at it."

"Extraordinary!" said the man again.

"So, Mr. Murphy, perhaps we should talk in the kitchen."

"Of course, Mr. Purcell, of course." Phonse stood and turned to the diners. "Excuse us," he said with a courtly bow.

Once through the kitchen doors, Phonse broke into a fit of laughter. "Dave, old man," He choked back a giggle. "It's extraordinary."

Dave took him by the arm and dragged him into a corner.

"Very busy now, Phonse. What is it?"

"Of course, Dave, sorry to disturb you. Isn't it something out there? People really seem to be having a bang-up time of it. And the grub, Dave, they love it. What did I tell you?"

More than simply being right, Phonse was responsible for the busy dining room. The bird caper was essentially his idea, and if he hadn't followed up Dave's bungled phone call to the radio station, it would have gone nowhere. Dave was worried that Phonse would someday ask for a favor in return, that he was observing the restaurant's success to take measure of what he was owed.

"Dinosaur bones, Phonse?" It had just struck Dave what Phonse had been telling his customers.

"Oh, that. Nothing yet, a new project. I actually came over to inquire whether you had an opportunity to —" Phonse glanced over his shoulder and discreetly pointed to his nose, "to get a price on the cocaine, you know, from your friend Larry."

Christ, thought Dave, remembering why Phonse had given him the heavy bag.

"I'm sorry, Phonse, I've just been swamped and —"

"Not to worry, not to worry, just curious. No pressure, Dave, no pressure at all. You want to proceed carefully, I'm sure, delicate matter and all."

"Do you need the money?" Dave asked. If he kept nipping down to the wine cellar for a boost there wouldn't be any sample to show anyone.

"No, no, not at all, just looking at a few last modifications on the R.S.V. before the testing phase and —"

"Because if you need some money, Phonse, I'd be more than happy to . . ." Dave saw an opportunity to settle with Phonse.

"No! Dave, not at all."

"I mean, Phonse, really I owe you."

"Not at all, Dave. What are friends for? I wouldn't expect any less of you."

It was certain, then, Phonse would someday come and ask for Dave's help in another, far more diabolical scheme. It was like striking a deal with the Mafia, once you were in, you were in for life.

The kitchen door opened and Alice entered from the dining room. She scowled at the two of them. "A fish stew, a leek torte and pasta," she said coolly.

"Got it, Alice," said Dave.

Alice shot Dave another stern look and returned to the dining room.

"I know this isn't the best place to talk, Dave, but I don't like using the phone." Phonse's voice dropped to a conspiratorial whisper. "The Winnebagos." He winked and headed for the back door. "How are you, Bet?" he asked on his way out.

"I'm fine, Mr. Murphy, how are you?"

"Extraordinary, Bet," Phonse said and was gone.

Dave leaned against the wall. It would soon be payback time. He had made a pact with the devil. Bet was looking at him with what Dave took to be pity in her eyes.

"Want for me to get the fish stew, Mr. Purcell?"

"Please, Bet, please," said Dave.

9

Dave's butcher in St. John's was Maher's, downtown on Water Street. The Maher boys, now in their sixties, had taken over the business from their father, who had inherited it from his. They were huge puddings of men, the way butchers were supposed to be, sent to this earth by a cosmic central casting, a comforting cliché. In the fall of the year a brace of rabbits hung above the door as an invitation, and generous light streamed through the big front windows. Scrawled across these windows, in a fat butcher hand, were soap letters announcing local pork chops, salt beef by the tub, Maher's store-made sausages, moose dressed and packaged — "You Shoot." The floor was covered with blood-gathering sawdust. Orders were wrapped in brown paper and tied with string. People didn't just come to Maher's to pick up their meat, they came to talk, to tell tales and to gossip. You could still smoke there.

The latest generation of Maher "boys" running the shop were three girls. They handled the counter while big

Billy and Paul stayed in the back working the saws and coolers. Dave loved to see the old fellows emerging from behind the heavy doors with great hunks of meat slung over their shoulders, their mass towing frosty, blood-scented gusts into the shop.

Being a major customer, Dave was afforded the privilege of coming in the back, dealing directly with the uncut animals, getting to slap at the carcasses, squeeze the flesh, flirt with the meat.

When Billy Maher, his broad bottom resting on a big white plastic tub of pickled pork riblets, saw Dave come in the door, a wide carnivorous smile crossed his face.

"Dave Purcell, where have you been all these months?"

"Laying low, Billy."

The bulky man had responded with a great store-shaking bellow of laughter. "You've been laying low, have you!"

He always laughed like this at whatever Dave said. He and his brother and their daughters were always happy. The health experts could say what they liked about meat, about how it would kill you, but it sure made people happy. Grinding poverty, the six-cent-a-day dole still played on Newfoundland's collective unconscious and meat meant prosperity.

Dave needed seven lambs, the best, fatty animals from the Cape Shore. Billy responded to the request as he always did, by solemnly shaking his head, saying they could barely keep up with the orders they already had, that he had nine pigs to carve up by the end of the day, a truck arriving with sides of beef to unload and not a sausage in the shop. He insisted that it was impossible to fix Dave up with his lambs on such short notice. Dave said that he was desperate. Billy said he would do what he could and to come back in an hour.

Dave returned and his lambs were ready.

He went from Maher's to Knickle's. Madame Knickle — Dave didn't know her first name, she had never volunteered it — operated a very chichi gourmet boutique in a plaza not far from Larry Doyle's neighborhood. It was an austere, severe temple of food. Here Dave acquired rare and precious ingredients — his truffles, fresh and preserved foie gras, caviar and *confit* — all dispensed with the cautious measure of an apothecary.

Love (Madame Knickle had married a local author of little note) had brought her to St. John's from Strasbourg. Finding her new home desperately lacking many of life's necessities, she opened the shop. It was her contribution to the effort undertaken by many foreign residents, Canadians included, to make their penitential exile in the distant outpost just that little bit more bearable.

In her boxy suit, her hair perfectly coiffed, Madame Knickle greeted Dave with a formality that set the tone, hushed and reverential, for the shop.

"It's zo very good to zee you again, Mr. Purcell. How may I be of azzistance today?"

She filled Dave's order promptly and, with an unconcealed grimace, accepted his cheque.

"Bon appétit," she said as he left.

While acquiring good meat and French delicacies was always a pleasure, getting fresh vegetables in St. John's was an ordeal, a torture for anybody who cared about food.

They were shipped to Newfoundland in dubious condition and always arrived near the end of their usefulness. Only in August and September was high-quality local produce available. The rest of the year Dave was forced to go to the wholesaler's warehouse in Fort Pepperell, an old American military base in the city's east end, to dig through the boxes as they were slung out the back of the refrigerated trucks. It was a treasure hunt, examining crate after crate of yellowing compost in search of the occasional green leaf or a wax bean with a crunch. It took too much of his time and usually left Dave in a surly mood.

But not this day. Dave felt wonderful driving the packed Skoda back to the Auk. He was happy to be engaged, to be busy again, to have returned to his true purpose in life.

From the parking lot Dave could hear music. Rossini. La Danza — a tarantella was rattling the building. He walked to the front windows and spied Alice in the dining room. She was dancing as she set the tables for lunch. She snapped out a fresh linen tablecloth as though it were a toreador's cape. She pressed a handful of cutlery to her breast in mock distress. She began to pump her hips forward in time to the music. Dave moved to the side of the window to better hide himself and peeped round the frame. How far would he go, he wondered, how much would he watch? If she was bathing, if she was asleep, would his attention become perverse? Now his hips, too, were grinding, against the wall of the

Auk. In sympathy to the music or wishfully in concert with Alice? He stepped away from the window, feeling ashamed of himself.

When Dave walked into the dining room from the kitchen, she was no longer dancing but setting the tables in the most routine fashion, completely ignoring the rhythm of the music, now Verdi.

After unpacking the supplies, Dave went to his apartment to shower and get ready for another busy day in the kitchen. The presence of Alice and Bet at the Auk was reassuring. They were both so competent. And Alice had hired two more waitresses. Young women from Push Through. She familiarized them with the menus and the wine list. She took care of their pay. The new women still called him Mr. Purcell but took their orders from Alice, who was proving she knew more about running a restaurant than Dave ever would. He thought he was very lucky. If not for the efforts of Phonse and Alice, he would be spending another lonely day licking his wounds.

He was completely undressed, heading for the shower, towel in hand, when the phone by his bedside rang.

"Hello, the Auk."

"Hello, David."

"Claire!"

"Are you still answering the phone that way? I thought you had shut down."

"That was only a temporary measure. Business is booming, dear."

"Really, that's . . . that's great." Claire didn't sound as though she believed him. "What happened?"

"It's a very strange story. A rare duck was spotted in the area."

"A duck, Dave?"

"Yes, Tasker's sulphureous. Terrifically rare. Anyway, we're full of bird-watchers."

"It's an odd time of the year for a duck, isn't it?"

"Apparently they're just returning from the south. How are you, Claire?"

"Honestly, Dave, I'm miserable."

This was a surprise. Had Claire decided she missed Dave? "What's wrong?" he asked.

"My schedule is brutal. I'm calling from Toronto, actually. I'm here giving a talk."

Dave stiffened. Toronto was close. An easy three-hour plane trip and she was back.

"And I'd love to come down for a quick visit, but they've scheduled me in for a panel discussion thing in San Francisco and then I've got a two-day session with my agent in New York. I'm going to be reinvented, apparently."

"Reinvented?" Dave couldn't remember Claire having an agent.

"My image. My agent thinks I should soften it. There's a feeling in Washington that the pendulum is due to swing back to the left. I mean, really, how many people can they put in prison? I was starting to get uncomfortable with all these right-to-lifers anyway. I'm so disappointed that I'm not going to be able to get down to see you."

To his great shame Dave felt relieved. "Oh, Claire. It's getting to be a long time." Saying this made him feel worse.

"I'm sorry, Dave, I am. But that's great news about the restaurant."

"Yeah, it's wonderful. Maybe all is not lost for the Auk."

"I was talking to Moira." Claire was changing the subject, no longer wanting to encourage false hopes about the restaurant. She was no doubt going to bring up Dave's atrocious behavior at their friends' home.

"Yeah?" asked Dave, waiting for Claire to suggest he get help.

"Things with her and Larry aren't very good, you know. I think maybe you should have them up for dinner."

"I was down there just the other day."

"Really? Moira never mentioned that. I think it may have something to do with Larry's work. He's so busy and traveling so much . . . I know! You should have Moira up sometime when Larry's out of town."

"I will," said Dave, knowing full well that he wouldn't.

"I'm going to get back very soon, David. I promise. I think we really need to spend some time together to sort things out."

This was it, thought Dave, she was going to ask for the divorce.

"I think that's a good idea, Claire. You know where to find me."

"Let's be civil, David."

"I was being civil. I meant it."

"You were being sarcastic. You haven't come down to visit me in Washington, have you?"

"I will. As soon as I can get someone to run the restaurant, I'm on a plane."

"Really. That would be great," Claire said. Dave could detect insincerity. "Let's make sure it's a week I'm in town."

"Okay."

"Dave, I've got to go. I'm going to speak in an hour and honestly I haven't a clue what I'm going to say. I miss you."

Why did she say *that*? She was obliging Dave to lie in response. He thought for a moment that he wouldn't do it.

"I miss you too, honey," he said.

"Gotta go. I'll call."

"Bye."

"Bye."

She hung up.

What forces had pulled them apart, flung them about the globe to distances beyond the range of the heart? Hadn't Dave encouraged Claire to vigorously pursue the career that had taken her to Washington? Like any good liberal sap, he wasn't going to be the man that stood between his wife and success. But he saw now that what Claire once identified as her personal project in the greater cause of feminism, was nothing more than naked ambition, utterly devoid of ideology. And what was wrong with that? Couldn't Claire simply be driven? The problem, he knew, was that his wife's ambition presented a troubling mirror to his own lack of incentive, his lethargy. Where Claire *wanted*, Dave just *was*. Yet Dave still felt, hiding somewhere inside him, a love for Claire. Didn't he? No, that was the problem, he didn't *feel* it, he *thought* it. He had a completely intellectual response to his wife. He knew why he should love her, but could not make his heart respond to reason.

When they first met, sex and romance were not an issue. They were young — there was sex and romance enough for all. Their lives had been full of flings and hasty drunken trysts quickly forgotten. That they should have to rely on one another, exclusively, for passion did not occur to them when they married. In their twenties, sex was a constant act of discovery. They learned more and more every day. Sex got easier and easier, fulfillment certain, and it seemed it would continue to reveal itself forever. But somewhere through the years, it became more complicated, the truth of the act more cryptic, harder to fully comprehend, until it had again become a puzzle.

It was so with all things, Dave thought. The world and its workings revealed themselves until they became an absolute mystery.

He did not know why, but stepping into the shower, he believed the woman dancing upstairs in the dining room of his restaurant understood the mystery.

10

By June the Auk was all the rage. Getting a table at the smart little restaurant by the sea was considered a minor social coup. Bigwigs in the oil business, politicians and even visiting celebrities had their handlers make peculiar inquiries about late reservations, declarations dressed up as requests. "Mr. Bowie has heard about your restaurant and would very much like to dine this evening." At first Dave was caught off guard by the sudden status of his tiny restaurant and was obliged to turn away the likes of the premier of Ontario and, more regrettably, The Tragically Hip, who were giving a concert in St. John's. The place was becoming one of the few things around damp old Newfoundland that could be called exclusive. Dave learned to always hold back a table, if not for a visiting celebrity or a highly placed politician, then to be awarded at the last minute to a grateful latecomer.

The foodies returned. Dave now distinguished two schools of gastronomy. The avant-garde were a chatty crowd, middle-aged enthusiasts who went in for innovative technique, admiring the architectural construction of a meal as much as its taste and aroma. They celebrated collisions of unlikely ingredients and dishes requiring structural-engineering skills — spans of lemongrass and daikon cantilevers — to keep them propped up on the plate. Food for them was a dalliance, an entertainment. They decided the Auk was a success if only because what was old seemed, after all the fads, new again.

The old school, the traditionalists, ate in silence, eschewed experimentation and any wine from the new world. They measured a meal by its command of the basics: béarnaise was béarnaise and it was either prepared properly or inedible. They came to the Auk like they were coming home.

The Auk's good fortunes enabled Dave to hike up prices a couple of notches to the point where the restaurant should finally have been profitable — but the consequent increase in revenue gave him the confidence to take a rather cavalier attitude to wine acquisition. With the addition of extravagant bottles, the restaurant's wine list was growing heavy in the hands. Venerable and rare '61s and big '82s from Bordeaux, auction-piece '78s from Burgundy. Haughty aristocrats from the likes of Latour, Richebourg and Vega Sicilia were the new lords of the dark stone room in the basement. These merit badges in wine snobbery were so obscenely expensive that the only people ordering them had too much money to know any better. It was folly.

Dave was spending more and more time in the cellar, ostensibly to keep the burgeoning wine collection in order, but in fact to service his cocaine habit. Despite the occasional panic attack over the rapidly diminishing weight of his stash, Dave knew his little indulgence was under control, never binging, just "chipping." Three or four lines to get him through the night, five, six or seven if the kitchen was particularly trying that day. No more than ten, though, even in the event of a major crisis. There had been several crises, the more serious involving customers having run amok.

Among the glitterati who had visited the Auk, none was so frequent a customer as Harry Todd, a local boy who had gone on to television fame, the jovial clown of a comedy troupe called The Package. The good life had taken its toll on Harry. His face showed signs of big-time boozing: weighty sagging bags hung under his eyes and a delicate tattoo of broken capillaries decorated his nose. His waistline had expanded exponentially from season to television season. Alice informed Dave that Harry was constantly whining about his weight during the meals, but that he was being forcefully encouraged to finish his servings by his manager, a hyperactive svengali named Gerry Fifield. Fifield kept insisting that "fat is funny." "John Candy, Oliver Hardy, Jackie Gleason, W.C. Fields — come on, Harry, face it, fat is funny. They didn't call him Fatty Arbuckle for nothing, you know. Now finish your pasta." Alice told Dave that Harry would sometimes be quietly sobbing as he stuffed his face.

At the end of one particularly caloric meal Todd jumped from his chair holding a table knife to his throat. At first Alice and the startled diners had imagined that Harry was planning to slash his jugular, but it became clear when Dave came from the kitchen and attempted to calm the comic, that Harry was, in fact, threatening to undertake a bit of hasty cosmetic surgery by hacking at one of his many chins.

The stand-off lasted a long twenty minutes. Business wasn't much affected. The other diners kept ordering drinks, as if at some cabaret, while the drama played itself out. They seemed entirely entertained by the histrionics, the plaintive sobs, the promise of bloodshed. They expected this from "show people." A woman at one table offered that Harry's taking his own chin hostage was vastly better than anything he had done during his last couple of seasons on television. The truce finally came when manager Fifield promised Harry that he would get him his own special on CBC-Television, with a lineup of guests that were all more obese than Harry. Not only that, Fifield also committed to sending the big man to the most exclusive fat farm and liposculpting boutique in Arizona to reduce for the cameras. When Harry finally set down the knife and embraced Fifield, a cheer went up from the other tables.

The second major incident of the spring did not have such a happy ending. Two huffing, puffing, red-faced birders, a German couple, crashed screaming into the restaurant kitchen late one foggy morning. In their search for the rare duck, they had spotted, in the sea, swirling and rolling at the command of the surf, a body. The police and ultimately the coast guard were summoned to retrieve the drowned woman. They plucked the poor unfortunate from the cold water at the bottom of a cliff not half a mile up the coast from the restaurant. Dave was obliged to answer police questions about the habits of the birders, how they had come to frequent the area, what possessed them to take such risks and so on. Having grown squeamish in middle age, Dave watched the recovery of the body from a distance. He would never know for sure, but the lifeless water-weighted lump that was hauled into the coast guard Zodiac seemed to him to be the goofy English woman he found in the bushes outside his restaurant on the very day he and Phonse had planted the seeds of the bird fraud. So now it was murder, or at least criminal negligence causing death.

The poor woman had been crawling the cliffs in search of a fiction concocted by Dave and Phonse, only for her own doleful chapter to end in death. Dave imagined her picking her way along the slippery rocks, pressing her chubby face against the back of a long-lensed camera, stepping backwards to adjust her composition, situating some grebe or grosbeak or osprey handsomely off centre, losing her footing and the bird jumping from the frame, her pretty picture becoming irritated blurs and streaks of blue, green, gray and white, her round head thrown hatless and dashed frightfully clear of sense against a cruel spear of granite, bouncing once or twice more against the cliff face before plunging into the numbing water, frigid enough to sting her, briefly, back into consciousness, giving her a moment to witness her own terror at drowning.

Dave was seized with such remorse that he contemplated confession. He was only dissuaded from doing so by Phonse. Morbid Phonse had been intrigued by the accident, going to a spot along the cliffs past the Auk to get as near the body as he could to examine it. He assured Dave that it was not the English woman. Even though he had never seen her, Phonse insisted that the body did not meet the description Dave offered. Dave doubted him.

Phonse had asked, "Glasses?"

"Yes."

"Then it's not her," said Phonse.

"Plump?" asked Dave.

"Thin," said Phonse.

"She looked plump from here," said Dave.

"She was full of water," said Phonse.

Phonse could not understand how Dave connected the misinformation they had planted in the minds of the birders with the accident. In Phonse's universe "everybody took their chances." For Phonse, the woman at the bottom of the cliff had simply run out of luck. If it wasn't falling into the sea, she would have been run over by a bus or struck by lightning or would have choked on a bone in Dave's restaurant and wouldn't that be a fine mess. Dave needed to accept this reasoning.

Still, Dave's guilt over the accident was such that he hastily painted and posted signs warning SEAS AND CLIFFS IN THIS AREA ARE EXTREMELY DANGEROUS. PROCEED WITH CAUTION. He borrowed the wording from signs at Cape Spear. Looking at his efforts some days after the drowning, Dave realized that he hadn't taken full account of the perils of Push Cove and that he should have added: ASSOCIATIONS WITH PERSONS FROM THIS AREA MAY WELL BE YOUR UNDOING. TALK WITH NO ONE.

Yet another crisis involved Larry Doyle. Once the Auk became *the* spot to dine and in which to be seen, Larry was always on Dave to squeeze him in. Larry, even though he was flush with the plunder of consultancy, could ill afford to eat at such an expensive restaurant so often. He would drag a fatigued and reluctant Moira to the Auk along with some associates from the Fisheries Department, young jerks unknown to Dave, and make much of his friendship with the owner, suggesting to his guests, according to the ever-attentive Alice, that he got preferential treatment from the kitchen. Dave was finding it so aggravating that he once deliberately made a mess of Larry's order, tossing sugar in Larry's five-mushroom soup and generously spraying his lobster in black bean sauce with raspberry vinegar. Alice said that Larry pronounced the soup "nonpareil, the mushrooms almost sweet" and the lobster "wonderfully tart, full of life, the black beans bringing out the berry-like character of the lobster roe that Dave uses to thicken the sauce."

"He isn't just saying it, Dave," Alice had astutely observed, "he believes it. He's having such a good time just being here, bullshitting his guests, that it actually tastes good to him. It tastes like success."

This aspect of the restaurant's life distressed Dave. After a certain point, he thought, if the prices were high enough and tables scarce enough, he could serve up steaming plates of shit. The rich would go in for it, they loved to be humiliated. Passionate physical appetites, the devotion to food, the full appreciation of its smell, its texture, its fire and certainly its primary function as sustenance did not motivate the fashionable crowd now frequenting the Auk. Their relationship with food was pained; eating, filling the mouth, chewing was always somehow vulgar. Eating made one belch and fart. It gave you bad breath, became, in the end, only unsightly fat and foul excreta. Cultivated people could have passing fancies for the newest dish, the latest national cuisine, this season's green, but true devotion to food was altogether too naked, letting oneself go, a very public lust.

Larry also had an irritating habit of strolling into the holy realm of the kitchen, desecrating it while Dave was frantically filling orders, so he could introduce some new acolyte.

"Gilbert, I'd like to introduce my good friend Dave Purcell, a refugee from Fisheries." Larry would chuckle at this and inevitably stick his finger in some sauce to sample it. Dave was sure that Larry was telling the lads at the department that he was a silent partner in the Auk.

The top blew when Larry showed up one night, unannounced, with a svelte woman in her twenties, a cool, sleek Montrealer, with an impossible head of copper hair, squeezed into a tube dress of some pornographic new synthetic. She was, Larry whispered, from the minister's office in Ottawa. It was critical that Larry get a table at the Auk if he was to further his interests with the department and, for a trophy, fuck the young creature. Dave was shocked, and asked after Moira and the twins. Larry assured Dave that he and Moira were finished, that they hadn't had sex in years, that he suspected Moira had gone dyke on him.

Dave knew that it was his own desire for Alice, his own shame at entertaining thoughts of cheating on his wife, that precipitated it, but he threw Larry out. He could have simply told Larry the truth, that there was no table to give him, but instead he lectured Larry, said he was disgusted with him and that he never wanted to see him back at the restaurant. Larry was taken aback and was almost apologetic until, as he was weaving his way through the restaurant to the front entrance, Dave came out of the kitchen to shout after him, "Have some respect for your wife, man!"

Larry, disgraced in front of the other diners, yelled back at Dave something to the effect that he and Moira had propped Dave up when he was at his lowest point and that Dave, now successful, was too self-centered to show any gratitude. Larry concluded by saying, "If it wasn't for that goddamn duck out there, you would have been bankrupt by now."

It was a disaster. The elusive duck was mentioned and Alice, serving a table at the time, heard Dave preach the merits of fidelity. There was trouble on both fronts.

The twitchers, the crowd interested only in their ornithological score cards, their lists, had, as predicted, arrived in droves. They were not a dining lot. They ate at the restaurant reluctantly, grumbling about the prices and expressing doubts as to the existence of the rare bird. Their parsimony was at odds with the enormous sums they had dished out to travel to Newfoundland to see a duck. Out and out twitcher revolt was averted only by the arrival of the caplin in the bay below the restaurant. The tiny fish came to the beaches by the millions every June to spawn, attracting whales and seabirds. The twitchers, while missing Tasker's sulphureous, got to list the goofy puffin and some rarely seen shearwaters and storm petrels — as consolation.

The experts also showed. They didn't dine at all, preferring to munch on desperate rations while clinging to the sea-sprayed rocks in their painfully earnest, methodical, scientific search for the duck. Luckily for Dave, the experts could never come to any conclusion about whether the bird still existed. They divided into opposing camps: those believing in Hans Speidel and thus the existence of the duck; and the nay-sayers, putting the recent anonymous report of a sighting down to an amateur's inevitable error in observation. It was rumored that Dr. Speidel, though near death somewhere in Bavaria, was to visit the site and that his arrival would cause the bird to miraculously appear. That men of science should harbor a belief that the great ornithologist had the power to invoke an extinct duck surprised Dave. But then at Fisheries he had witnessed scientists reinterpret and re-evaluate data, squeezing it while clicking voodoo chicken lips at it, until they had conjured thousands of tons of fish from the bottom of a barren sea.

Dave was again feeling the fear that had permeated the department when the fish stocks collapsed. The beast of worry, the sleep thief was coming back. Those searching for the bird were growing disillusioned and they were still the core of his trade. If they were to abandon the search as the summer faded, the Auk would lose its critical mass. The people who found it important to dine at a restaurant where reservations were difficult to obtain would stop coming and it would be like March all over again.

Meanwhile, Dave made little progress with Alice. Claire's calls were becoming more frequent. She knew, likely by talking to her old girlfriends in St. John's, that the fortunes of the Auk had taken a turn for the better. At first Claire subtly pressured Dave to sell it while business was good, to increase her booty from the divorce, Dave supposed, but she soon dropped this idea. Dave guessed that Claire heard from her spies that the Auk was becoming one of the rare spots where the few people who mattered in St. John's could be seen, and so thought the restaurant might be an effective tool in her networking arsenal. She wasn't stupid, she would keep her options open, she would have a Plan B that entailed a return to Newfoundland once the States was engulfed in a full-scale race war. Worse still, Claire was warming to Dave, attracted to his success, seeing him now as an appealing combination of manservant and novelty piece ("Why don't we go to my restaurant. I'll call ahead and have Dave put together something special"). If she returned, Claire would be entitled to her own table at the Auk, where she would take lunch after lunch, calling for Dave to open his treasured bottles, pouring for her privileged guests.

In the face of all these phone calls, Dave was feeling increasingly guilty for wanting Alice. The phone calls served as a constant reminder to the object of his desire that her chubby boss was hitched. Dave would often grumble about Claire so that Alice could overhear him, but Alice didn't seem to care, never once expressing sympathy for his marital plight. And the more time he spent in Alice's company, the more he studied her slender strength, the more his eyes found hers across the room, the more he watched her step from the heat of the kitchen into the cool of a summer night to stretch her weary back like a cat, the more her lips parted with laughter or even a sigh and changed the very nature of the air, the more he loved her. The more he loved Alice the more mute he became. He had begun wanting her and now wanted to be had by her, wanted to be her pet, her dog. His longing was desperate. When she entered the room his blood would rise so that he could hear it, noisily rushing through his head, his veins crying from loneliness and desire.

Dave could never speak to Alice about his feelings for her, but so craved her voice that he made nightly inquiries about her life. After the restaurant emptied they would share a drink in the kitchen, where Alice, with every answer to Dave's queries, would draw him deeper into her spell. She had abruptly dropped out of a doctoral program in anthropology at McGill when a long affair with a professor had turned sour. She had since become interested in the study of architectural photography. After Montreal there had been a couple of short and inconsequential flings so that she now felt perfectly content being alone. The few friends she had in St. John's were too busy with their kids or their work to see her very often. She could no longer bear visiting her home town of Gull Tickle, finding it a horribly depressing place since the collapse of the fisheries. A voracious and indiscriminate reader, she strongly recommended a memoir by Anatole Bruyard entitled *Kafka was the Rage*. Movies mostly disappointed her. Until she had been busied and drained by her work at the Auk, she had gone swimming every day. She wanted to visit Italy, but couldn't afford it. (Dave thought she looked somehow Italian.) She was suspicious of her brother-in-law, for he had too many secrets, but knew that her sister was deeply in love with the man. She had never been deeply in love with anybody. She enjoyed working at the Auk ... "For now!" She didn't like sweets, never took dessert, and had a man's taste for onion, garlic and anchovy, but did enjoy sweet wine, unctuous Sauternes and creamy Loires. She didn't really have any plans.

Did she know that she had Dave's heart, that she had taken it from him and kept it now locked in a box, a box she had buried somewhere along the woody path leading from the Auk to the fortress in which she slept?

11

Success let Dave blithely forget his dark spring. By July he had completely put from his mind the duplicity that had changed his fortunes and the debt owed his partner in crime, Alphonse Murphy. But Mr. Murphy kept a strict ledger.

The day of reckoning dawned hot as an oven. Returning from his daily St. John's grocery run, Dave saw that even the car wreckers of the Upper Road and their patchy hounds had retreated to the shade. Dave was pulling into the Auk's parking lot when a severe-looking Phonse emerged from the bushes. Dave parked the heavily laden little car and got out to greet his neighbor.

"Phonse."

"Need your assistance, Dave." Phonse scanned the area, likely for the Winnebagos. "I'm ready for sea trials. I'd like to rendezvous at oh-three-hundred hours in my shed. I'll fill you in later."

Dave could not think of a way out. Genetically predisposed to wilt in the sun, he could barely think at all. Sweat was burning his eyes, briny rivulets filling the crevices and canyons of his nether regions. Phonse, despite wearing a jacket, heavy cotton work pants and boots, was not affected by the unnatural heat.

"And Dave?"

"Yes, Phonse?"

"Try not to be seen. Winnebagos."

With that Phonse was gone, disappearing back into the bush with a bouncy trot, the trees folding around him, an animal native to the terrain. It was payback time. But what had Phonse really done for him? Simply placed a phone call. The geezer was certainly getting the better of the deal. Dave would probably be required to paint his face with shoe polish, wear night-vision goggles and carry a weapon to be of any assistance to Phonse. There would be blood ceremonies and vows of secrecy. Dave was imagining the picture, more pathetic than frightening, as he entered the kitchen.

Alice and Bet fell silent as the door swung open.

"What's up, girls?" Dave deposited several bags of turnip greens on a counter.

"Nothing, Dave," answered Alice, a little scarlet appearing high on her cheeks. Alice never blushed, her voice never wavered, she never expressed any doubt or embarrassment whatsoever.

And then Bet giggled, giggled and quickly shuffled to a sink to busy herself.

"Nothing's up, hey?"

"You look exhausted, Dave."

Dave knew Alice was trying to divert him, to stop him

from prying, but with her question Dave suddenly did feel terrifically shagged. Perhaps it was that Gull Tickle black magic at work. Alice was "thinking on" some long dead ancestor, channeling maleficent energies from beneath the earth into Dave's skull. Perhaps it was only his anxiety at having to tangle with Phonse in the wee hours that was sapping him.

"I am tired, Alice."

"Your wife called." Dave had to sit down. Alice continued. "She's planning on coming up sometime soon, maybe in August."

"Oh, shit." Dave suddenly felt fluish. His muscles ached.

"She was kind of curt with me."

Dave put his head in his hands, testing its weight, confirming it was made of stone. What was happening? All his strength was leaving him, he felt as though he had been jabbed by a narcotic needle. He would have to call a doctor.

"I don't know, Dave, but . . ." Alice was shifting her weight from foot to foot, uncharacteristically stammering. "Well . . . I think she suspects we're having an affair."

"If only," Dave said.

He listened as his words filled the kitchen. *If only*. He had, in a moment of weakness, betrayed his secret desire. Distracted, agitated, put upon, possibly even hexed, he had confessed that he wanted to make love to the woman who had just informed him of his wife's plan to come home.

Dave looked at the floor, unable to look up, desperately trying to figure a way out of the situation, a means of turning the simple two-word phrase into something harmless. The seconds slipped away beyond the point where he could add crucial words, change the meaning, "if only... she would come in September" or "if only... she didn't have to be so suspicious." More seconds evaporated. Too late to make Alice believe she hadn't heard it quite right by repeating something sounding like "if only," Dave's mind raced to construct credible possibilities: "I phonely... I phoned Troy... I fondly remember those days in Botwood ... I've only got turnip greens."

"And Hans Speidel is arriving tonight," said Alice.

Dave was baffled.

"The big bird guy, the German guy who's big on the duck."

Alice rescued him, let the revelation of desire slip by as if it had never been said. She wasn't going to punish him for having said it, she wasn't going to walk out in a huff, complain of sexual harassment in the workplace. She was going to let him off the hook.

"Right, Speidel. Jeez we should give him one on the house."

"He'll be here around eleven o'clock this evening. They're coming straight from the airport. Twelve of them for something light and drinks, a sort of reception. I told them it would be okay. I know it's late but it's almost like a third seating. A little gravy."

It was impossible for Dave to protest. Alice lingered, stepping toward him and laying a hand on his shoulder. It was a maternal gesture, her touch filling Dave with comfort, inducing sleepiness. Their bodies had collided in the course of work, but this contact was deliberate and full of warmth. It seemed more forgiveness than an invitation.

"Get a nap, Dave. It's going to be a big night. You should think about closing the joint for a couple of nights next week, Monday and Tuesday, get some serious rest," Alice said and left to set tables.

Dave was playing a perilous game, filling his empty tanks with cocaine, forcing himself into turbid slumber with bedtime cocktails of codeine and cognac, jump-starting the mornings with clenched fists of aspirin and espresso, taking the edge off at lunch with a couple of lines and a quick beer. This program of abuse, not eating regularly and then binging, first resulted in weight gain. He began puffing up, yeasty and sweet from the booze. But of late, Dave was beginning to lose pounds. Though he was still carrying a gut, his face was becoming gaunt and drawn, deep lines were digging in around his eyes, sinews known only to pathologists were surfacing, pressing against the underside of his skin. His gums pushed at his lips. He had to finish this dreadful day and commit to a period of recuperation, heal the system. It was time to mend.

He collapsed on the bed, too tired to think about Claire coming home, about the arrival of Dr. Hans Speidel, about the late-night rendezvous with Phonse, but somehow finding the energy to once more analyze Alice's reaction to his confession of desire. She had let it go. She hadn't seemed surprised. She had softly touched his shoulder. Was it an indication that he should continue to speak freely, that she would be responsive to his advances? He imagined his mouth meeting hers, kissing her deeply, pulling her tightly against him, feeling her taut body under his hands. They were standing in the woods, the Auk was burning in the distance, the dancing orange light casting cocky shadows with the trees...

"Dave! Dave! They're from Tourism, they said you're expecting them." Alice was shaking him.

He sat up on the bed but couldn't quite wake. He sensed something had gone wrong with time, couldn't place himself in the day.

"Bet and I decided to let you sleep." Alice was answering a question Dave couldn't remember asking.

"It was only lunch, I didn't think you would mind. You didn't look well this morning."

He got to his feet. "Tourists?"

"No." Alice was trying to catch his eye, craning her neck to make contact. "Tourism. The Department of Tourism."

"Yes." It was coming back to Dave, they were going to take pictures for pamphlets. He staggered slightly. "Tell 'em to go mad, take all the pictures they want." He leaned toward his pillow, ready to drop.

"Dave, the minister's up there."

"What?"

"Yes, the minister of tourism, with a half a dozen lackeys in tow. I don't think they're taking pictures today."

"Jesus suffering Christ."

"You better come up. Splash some water in your face or something. I'll show them around, give them a drink."

"Yeah, give them drinks. Good idea. Drinks. They'll like that."

Alice left.

Dave felt heavy from a sleep that had done nothing to restore him. In the bathroom mirror he saw why Alice had insisted on a wash. He looked like a bum. Hobo Dave. He filled the sink with cold water and submerged his face. The jolt brought some measure of clarity to his thinking.

That a day, this day, could be such a trial proved that Alice was right about closing up for a few days. "When I die, I'm going to heaven because I've already been to Wednesday" was not the motto of a man in full command of the situation. Alice and Bet had handled lunch, they could handle it again tomorrow. He would shut the place down tomorrow night until next Wednesday, there would be time enough to get back to the bookings and express regrets. He would concoct an excuse, renovations, or illness, anything. Why hadn't he taken on a second cook anyway? He was being unfair to himself. Dave needed only to get through this one day and then go for the big crash, get some perspective. He had earned it. And with a respite around the corner, it was hardly unreasonable to nip into the coke, just to get through this last hellish night.

Padding past the stairs in his fresh shirt and trousers, Dave could hear Alice and the government boys in the kitchen above. They were laughing at something she said. Probably all want to fuck her, thought Dave jealously as his step quickened, nearing the cellar.

He closed the door behind him. The cool darkness, the presence of his little bottled treasures, their internal glow settled him. It was the summer heat, for sure. He was suffering some kind of heatstroke. Once he retrieved his secret bag, he laughed out loud. Fuck it all. You only go around once. He was wasting his time with worry, becoming an old woman. With hands as quick as a magician's, he had a little pile of powder on a china dinner plate, a razor blade in his right hand and a straw in his left. The plate had a delicate blue glaze, a faint robin's egg color, which imparted a luminescence, a sickly cobalt glow, to the drug. He sectioned the pile into four parts when he could just as easily have chosen six and violently inhaled a great gob of powder. The effect was instantaneous. After a brief moment of concern over the condition of his nasal passage, thinking the rapid onset of the drug indicated that its corrosive action had, over the past months, burned a route through the cartilage and was acting directly on the brain, after a brief gasp and a fearful jump in his pulse, Dave was right again. Suddenly he wanted to talk to the minister. He felt perfectly charming.

Tourism. It was the last hope for Newfoundland, to become some kind of vast park, its people zoo pieces, playing either famished yokels or bit parts in a costume drama, a nation of amateur actors dressed up like murderous Elizabethan explorers, thrilling to the touch of their tights and tunics as they danced for spare change. It would never work. Nova Scotia was for tourists, a gentle, verdant land meeting the sea. What did they call it? "Canada's Ocean Playground." American Buddhists, middle-class followers of some lesser lama, Ginsbergs and Glasses, were flocking to Nova Scotia, to ring their little bells and drone their little chants. Nova Scotia was a good place to meditate. Newfoundland was a good place to repent — a thorny wilderness in which to wander. Newfoundland was *in* the sea, surrounded and tormented by its forces, at its mercy. Nova Scotia was predictable, the visitors got what they paid for. In Newfoundland they got a seven-hundred-pound moose appearing out of the fog and coming through the windshield at one hundred clicks an hour. Surprise! Dave met tourists all the time now and the site that most interested them was "that orphanage where all the little boys were abused by those priests, like in that miniseries." They were disappointed when Dave informed them that it had been torn down. What Newfoundland tourism needed, much more than a decent restaurant, was a ghastly waxworks of hiked black cassocks and splayed ivory limbs, a national bum-fucking museum.

There was no photographer. That would come later. First the minister of tourism and his delegation wanted to size up "the little restaurant that could." The minister, Heber Turpin, was the government member for Gashers–Beet Bay, an isolated and backward district, gerrymandered out of Newfoundland's Great Northern Peninsula. He was a coarse, burly fixer of the old school. With the Island's economy in free fall, there now seemed little benefit in holding office. There were scarce goodies left to dish out for the foreign industrialists and thus few opportunities to harvest a plump kickback or payoff. There was less and less competition for the prize of running the failing island, to get a piece of the phantom action.

Newfoundland was a tragic case. The political leadership of the country had once been great orators. They imagined that their land, the first British colony, a white colony, held some elevated position in the Empire. The debate as to whether the nation should join Canada, turn its back on the sea, on Europe, and attach its fortunes to the North American continent, had been stirring. It was only now becoming obvious that the final political decision was a mistake of appalling dimensions. Newfoundland had, in 1948, voted itself out of existence. The battered and bewildered nation, the sport of historic misfortune, the Cinderella of the British Empire, had ended its suffering by taking its own life.

Heber Turpin was not a noted orator. He was best known for having pitched a half-eaten donut across the floor of the provincial legislature, beaning the opposition whip with the deep-fried, chocolate-glazed confection. Such was contemporary political discourse in what the license plates decreed was Canada's Happy Province — Dave always thought a more appropriate slogan would have been "I forgets."

Dave introduced himself. The towering Turpin put his beefy arms around Dave's shoulders and squeezed.

"Mr. Purcell, this restaurant is a model for the service industry in Newfoundland." Turpin's handlers nodded silently, like pigeons.

Dave thanked him for the compliment. Alice brought the delegation a third round of drinks. Turpin's entourage seemed not to want any more booze, but the minister tossed half his tall scotch back in a single, loud gulp. What had happened to Newfoundlanders' common sense that they now elected such louts and dunderheads to political office? Lloyd had another theory that Newfoundlanders suffered a collective ignorance. The individuals of the country were sound of mind but as a group, they proved every bad Newfie joke true.

"Judas Priest, some of the food they are serving out there." Turpin lifted his chin, pointing it at an imagined horizon, improvising a speech. "We got every measure of nature lover and tree hugger now flocking to Newfoundland, and they are simply not equipped to deal with salt meat, pease pudding and pot liquor. They do not have the constitution, the digestive apparatus, to deal with grub better suited to a man who has worked in the lumber woods or on the water. Why, just the thought of eating a seal flipper can drive them to distraction."

Turpin turned back to Dave. "I am sure you've seen that, Mr. Purcell. You are acquainted with Canadians. I'll venture you have lived on the mainland. You've got that look about you."

"Yes, I spent a few —"

"But you are a Newfoundlander?"

"Yes."

"Thank God for that, would never do to have another come-from-away-makes-good story." Turpin's handlers laughed. The minister looked into his drink. It was evidently the source of his deepest thoughts.

The cocaine was enforcing several bizarre torments on Dave, one of which was the occasional tendency to focus, intensely and uncontrollably, on minute details

— determining a complex rhythm in the ringing of hidden plumbing late in the evening, studying the grain structure of wood, even paper. Now it was Turpin's body hair. On his huge mitts it was patterned in dense swirls. Great wiry clumps were sticking out of his ears. Dave could see a thick nest of the black strands up the minister's nose.

"I'll speak frankly, Mr. Purcell" — Turpin's handlers cringed slightly, sensing that their man was about to start a fire they would later have to extinguish — "Newfoundland has come to a fork in the road. One route will take us to tourism, eco-tourism I believe they say." Turpin scowled. "The other fork takes us to toxic waste disposal. You understand where I'm going?"

"I think so, Mr. Turpin." Dave had no idea.

"Call me Heber. The route to tourism is a long one, the route to toxic waste disposal a short one. We say yes and they're here with the waste in a week, and it's not as bad as it sounds, these people are serious industry, waste is big these days. But I suppose there are only so many holes to be filled in Newfoundland. The choice is hard. I say tourism is the industry of tomorrow."

Turpin's handlers relaxed, issuing a collective sigh.

"I like you, Dave. Can I call you Dave?" Turpin didn't wait for an answer. "I like your outlook and I appreciate your views on this matter."

Dave couldn't remember having expressed any views. He even wondered whether he had views any more. Life just seemed to be happening around him — events, personalities, the inevitable tears-and-gut-busting joke of it all, the very fiber of the swirling universe orbited Dave. He was a witness without an opinion, a participant without influence in all affairs.

"We have an advisory committee that I think ..." Turpin was talking to no one in particular since everyone's attention had been drawn to Alice, who had entered with a tray of lovely looking hors d'oeuvres. When had she prepared them? And where? They were all standing in the kitchen. She had managed lunch without him, had arbitrarily, over the past two months, made successful changes in the menu and now seemed to be orchestrating this little meeting. She had only woken Dave to avoid having to listen to Turpin, who was now wolfing down the tasty treats.

The cocaine was quickly becoming metal filings in Dave's mouth, an electric current ran itching between his teeth. The hors d'oeuvres were probably delightful, but the thought of eating one revolted him. Dave saw the ingredients reduced to their pure form — cheese was a pressed mass of curdled milk, otherwise delightful pâtés were the mashed organs of liver-bloated force-fed fowl, little crab cakes the gluey flesh of an ancient insect, even the crudités were twigs and roots, tubers, bark. He smiled, politely refusing as Alice passed the tray under his nose. Chef Dave, under the influence of the evil stimulant, had lost his appetite. He was too soon out of bed for a drink, but pushed through the gaggle of suits en route to the dining room and the bar where he poured himself a stiff scotch. Turpin was on his heels.

"To be truthful, I'm not the eating-out type myself, but your press is fantastic. First I heard of your restaurant was in one of those airplane magazines. Highly recommended." He held up a swollen vol-au-vent oozing creamy fish sauce. "Highly recommended! But now I can see what all the noise is about." Turpin popped the pastry in his mouth whole, like a gannet gobbling back a plump herring. Dave thought he saw a fine jet of saliva squirt out from between his closed lips. "Eeze are elicious." Dave took a drink while Turpin brushed some crumbs from his tie.

"And these bird freaks. Amazing, hey?" There was something conspiratorial in Turpin's tone. "Did you set up the restaurant out here because of that? I mean, Dave, who would think to open a restaurant in Push Cove? You are a shrewd one, hey? An operator." Turpin smiled, revealing little flecks of black olive flesh caught between his teeth.

"More of a happy accident, Mr. Turpin," said Dave.

"Is that so. Well, if the birds weren't here I'd say you would be wise to say they were anyway. I could talk to some people in Wildlife." Turpin winked.

Dave felt his neck heating up. From behind Turpin's olive-speckled grin came a swallowed belch of garlic and booze. The cursed bird again, he thought, reaching for the reservation book.

"Another busy one tonight," Dave said, trying to steer the conversation toward safer terrain.

Drunk, Turpin grabbed the book from Dave's hand and with some effort, focused his prying eyes on the names.

"Christ!" he snorted. "The names never change, do they? Elderidge, Nair, Platt. They're so inbred now that they all look alike. Have you ever noticed that? Not my social circle. I'm too crude for this lot. Old man Elderidge owned my hometown and everybody in it on the credit system. Now his smarmy offspring own the government." Turpin belched again. "I never said that, Dave. You know young Elderidge dresses up in women's underwear and takes it up the ass? Calls himself Lady Squires. Did you know that? It's a fact. Did you know that?"

"No, I didn't." Dave had to get away from Turpin.

"Cortini? What kind of a name is that?"

"Italian, I guess," answered Dave, noting the party of three on the list.

"You think, hey?"

"You'll have to excuse me, Mr. Turpin, but I've got to go to the cellar, get some wine. It's been a pleasure."

It worked. Ever the politician, Turpin extended his hand, like a trained seal. "Keep up the good work," he said as Dave fled.

He pushed through the suits in the kitchen shouting over his shoulder, "Sorry, I've got to get the wine ready for tonight." The excuse was probably satisfactory for the drink-flushed bureaucrats, but Alice would surely wonder how one got wine "ready."

Dave listened from the cellar, waiting for the delegation to depart. They stuck around for half an hour. By the time he headed back upstairs, he was five lines wiser and fuming. His calves ached from pacing the stone floor. Alice, too, was aggravated.

"Thank's a lot for leaving me with those losers, Dave!"

"You let them in," Dave said, retrieving a tray of pheasants from the fridge.

"It's not my job nor is it my restaurant. What is it with you?"

Dave realized he was moving too quickly, nervously chewing but with nothing in his mouth.

"I'm fried, Alice!" This was a confession of drug abuse. "You were right, I need a break."

"I'll say!" Alice went to work on the dinner preparation. She was trying hard to maintain her composure, but Dave could see she was seething.

"I'm sorry, Alice," he said. "I couldn't face them, not today. The evening's booked solid and with this late seating —"

"Is that my fault too?"

Dave was becoming Alice's boss. Scolding her for doing the right thing.

"No, Alice, it was a good idea." Dave couldn't lose her, not now.

The pace at dinner was merciless. The tables ordered the full range of the menu so there was no doubling up preparation. Dave enlisted Bet to stir sauces, toss salads, drain pasta, letting the dishes pile up until they started getting in the way. The night was balmy. Even with the back door open to the cool salt air off the bay, the kitchen was a sauna. Alice was tested to her limits, operating like a dancer in the dining room and a gymnast in the kitchen, rattling off orders while she dumped empty plates and glasses on any available surface, pirouetting around Dave like a circus act.

Time was so tight that Dave managed only two quick sprints to the cellar to rejuvenate himself, forgoing the plate and razor, filling his nostrils with burning gobs of powder straight from the bag.

He was sitting a pheasant atop a sauced plate when Alice, between a demand for a tournedos Rossini and a moules marinière, said, "Table of three is asking a lot of questions."

Dave paid it no mind until Alice, returning to the kitchen, mentioned it again. "Cortini, table of three, seems awfully curious, Dave."

Dave was on Alice's heels as she returned to the dining room. He scrutinized the Cortini table through the little window. It was a party of three straight-backed, stern men, looking uncomfortable. They were eating their food methodically, chewing as though Mom were watching, not talking to one another, surveying the room. There was no wine on the Cortini table. Dave cleared the swinging door as Alice strode into the kitchen.

"What kind of questions are they asking?"

"Another pheasant and a leek torte," said Alice.

"Bet, can you get up a leek torte?" Dave asked, still keeping his eyes on quick-moving Alice.

"Yes, Mr. Purcell." Bet was salvation.

"How long you've been open," Alice answered. "Is it always this busy? Do many people live in the area? Is there a proper wine cellar?"

"What!" Dave could have no one in his cellar, his sanctum and now, cache.

"And they didn't even order wine." Alice stopped for a second, considering this strange fact.

"Drinks?" Dave asked.

"Nothing, ice water," Alice answered, running a moistened blade through the Auk's celebrated chocolate hazelnut cake.

Dave returned to the window to observe the three men again. If they were having a business meeting, then they would surely be drinking, they would be telling testosterone tales, slapping backs, somebody would be selling or cajoling. Three men didn't dine at a good restaurant after a deal had collapsed. They could, of course, be alcoholics. Dessert would tell: reformed boozers always had an insatiable sweet tooth.

"Tell me what they order for dessert, Alice." He returned to the stove determined not to become alarmed. He busied himself with the tournedos Rossini. He put the gas to a skillet into which he poured clarified butter. He pulled back a blanket of wax paper from a tray to select a disc of beef, squeezing it, testing its temperature and strength with his fingers. The meat was cool, an odd comfort in the heat, the chill of dead flesh. People did not give enough consideration to what they ate, thought Dave, didn't pay homage to the creatures sacrificed for their pleasure. He dropped the tenderloin in the hot pan. It sizzled and recoiled.

Everyone in the dining room could be scrutinized, their motives questioned and found suspicious. How few people came to a restaurant merely to eat. The dining room was always full of seductions, hidden agendas, conspiracies being hatched. The low murmur of table chat from the dining room was carried on the music from the stereo, banalities on a bed of Prokofiev. He picked up the meat with tongs and turned it over, throwing a fistful of finely diced shallots in the pan.

Three men, not drinking and looking glum, were eating in his dining room. That was all he could say. There was nothing to worry about. Were they narcs? How could they be, unless Alice had figured out what was going on in the cellar and called them? It couldn't be poor Bet, unless she had been feigning her condition for all these years, part of some kind of intense deep-cover police operation. Perhaps Bet was in a hypnotic trance, only activated as an agent by a coded message, coming suddenly to her senses after years of living the life of a simpleton so she could spring into action to arrest Dave. Perhaps the mysterious men in the dining room were private detectives in Claire's hire. It would be like Claire to employ three of them.

When the tenderloin was almost cooked, Dave picked it up and placed it aside to rest. The pan continued to sizzle, the shallots just beginning to caramelize, turning amber then toasty brown. Dave added a healthy measure of Madeira to rescue the dark essence of meat and onion from the bottom of the pan. A powerful cloud of alcoholic vapors, smelling slightly of raisins, rose from the stove top. Having added a ladle of beef stock reduced nearly to syrup, he skipped across the floor to retrieve a plate from the warmer and laid it next to the stove. On the plate he placed six slivers of dark, earthy black truffle. The merging pan juices, stock and Madeira were boiling. He held a fine sieve, pouring the fluid from the pan onto the plate until the interior ridge was just covered. He placed the tournedos on the sauce and then a thick slab of foie gras on top.

With a spoon he drizzled the few remaining pan juices on the foie gras. Alice returned to the kitchen. He placed one perfect little rosemary-scented potato, roasted crusty, on the plate. Alice took the plate from Dave and, reaching into a cloud of steam, found three spears of white asparagus with which to finish the dish.

"Cortini table," said Alice.

"Yes."

"Don't want any dessert."

Alice must have noted Dave's apprehension. "It gets worse. Three coffees. One asked for decaf."

Decaf? It *was* time to worry.

The Cortinis took their fine time leaving, sipping no brandy, taking no second coffee, decaf or otherwise. They just sat there, watching the other customers finish and depart, tidily folding their napkins, examining their laps for crumbs. Dave checked on them no fewer than six times and only once did he see one of them say much, a couple of words and the response was nothing more than a nod. Dave could scarcely comprehend the discipline required to skip both the booze and the dessert. They were heavies, all right.

He would have jumped in the Skoda to follow them after they paid their bill if it wasn't for the arrival of the Speidel reception's lead party, two middle-aged men from the university. Clearly Speidel was held in some awe, for the two men insisted on twice reviewing the late-night buffet menu, nervous that everything should be just so.

Alice, perhaps feeling guilty for having taken the extra booking, handled most of the preparations for the buffet. The Speidel party could enjoy a tawny onion and beef soup. (Alice and Bet, taking wild liberties with Dave's precious stock, had made it earlier, while Dave slept.) There was tapenade, salt cod brandade, two lovely game pâtés en croûte, beautiful pink rainbow trout (served cold with a dill dressing) and a couple of salads. Hoping to make the German ornithologist feel at home, Dave dipped into his private supplies, digging out five prized Lunenburg sausages from the freezer. These had been braised in beer and were now sitting in a heated tray atop a steaming mound of Tancook sauerkraut. Both delicacies came from the south shore of Nova Scotia, an area settled by Speidel's countrymen. German, but more particularly Alsatian, cuisine, with its pork, sausage and cabbage, its Gewürztraminer, was a love of Dave's that had failed, as predicted by Alice, on the menu. People had a fixed image of the food they should eat at a restaurant, in public. It was a picture that did not include sausage, sauerkraut and dumplings. The colors were too earthy, lacking glamor, the shapes too organic, pornographic.

Dave went to the cellar to get a couple of bottles of Spätlese, two peppery Rhônes, four work-a-day clarets and a quick lift. He was opening the bottles in the dining room (Alice and Bet had pushed the tables against the walls in his absence) when the great Hans Speidel arrived. The two nervous advance men, whom Alice had fitted with settling drinks, rushed to the front door. Dave could hear a tremendous kerfuffle coming from the parking lot, there was a muffled grumbling and barked instructions. It was clear that there had been problems moving Speidel about. A good two hundred and fifty pounds of the man were in a wheelchair.

He wasn't, or hadn't been, a fat man, Dave could see, but what they called in Newfoundland "a big man," over six feet tall, barrel-chested, imposing. The loss of the use of his legs, his reliance on others, on bumblers and clods, seemed an indignity he could not well bear, so he snarled and elbowed and shook his head. His hair was a gray forest of erect bristles — the mad scientist prerequisite. Deep furrows were written in his forehead, a record of years of enforced concentration and recent physical pain, Dave supposed. But the fine features on the old man's face, the relationship of the watery gray eyes, the wide scowling mouth, the jutting chin, of this Dave and Alice could make only one observation. Speidel's face looked like Dave's. So much so that Dave was frozen, as though he had seen a ghost — his own.

A dozen twerps from the university were fighting to fetch a drink for a figure that Dave, his mind jagged from a night of visits to the cellar, saw as a direct message from God.

After having told the group what tasty delicacies were available and inviting them to serve themselves, Alice came to Dave, who hadn't moved an inch, who had just stood there with a corkscrew in his hand.

"Jesus, Dave, the geezer looks just like you, I mean if you were ninety."

"I see it, Alice. It's a message, a sign."

"You think?" Alice seemed amused by his dread.

"It *is*, Alice, you know I'm not superstitious but this..."

"I don't know much about you at all, Dave," Alice said. Was this true? Dave thought he had been completely open to Alice, that he had given too much away, leaving no mystery. He imagined that having been so transparent revealed how shallow he truly was. But Alice evidently suspected there was something more to Dave. She thought that the agitation, the paranoia, the abrupt retreats to the cellar were only surface. Alice was now just another person for Dave to disappoint.

Speidel's palate was exactly as Dave predicted. The old man's face eased out of its agonized frown when he tucked into the sausage and sauerkraut. And it was more than having guessed that the old man would find comfort in the food of home, it was the way he ate it, giving more attention to his plate than someone speaking to him, grinning, not at their words but, ridiculously, at a particularly enticing piece of sausage. This was Dave approaching his death. Only Dave would be alone, would die in an empty room. It would be days before anyone found the remains of the late Dave Purcell. No one would notice he was missing until the smell of all that rotting butter, cheese and sausage and sauerkraut teased a few nostrils. He would be alone and as ripe as a well-hung pheasant.

Someone handed Speidel a glass of the Spätlese, a VictoriaBerg, a sovereign wine. He slurped at it as Dave would have done, sloppily tasting and savoring, a little of the fluid ran down his chin, an oenophile in a trench coat, a wine pervert.

One of the Speidel party came to Dave.

"It's wonderful, the food. Thanks for having us on such short notice."

Dave wasn't hearing anything. He was trying to understand why fate had delivered this ghost to his restaurant. Was he being put on notice? Smarten up or you'll be old before your time! Death is closer than you think? Repent? Yes, repent, that was the message. And Dave would, he had made that promise to himself, after tonight, after this hellish night, after he was through with this tweedy lot and the messenger from Germany. Germany: the Second World War, Hitler, Nazis. Hadn't Göring been a drug addict?

The man was still talking to him. "Just so excited by it all, there aren't many happy endings in this business. But for a species thought extinct to make an appearance . . . It lifts one's spirits so."

This was too much. Dave Purcell was a prince among sinners.

"I'm sorry, you'll have to excuse me, I've got to go to the cellar. More Spätlese."

That Hans Speidel commanded such loyalty was at first a puzzle to Dave. The old man treated his followers (it seemed the right thing to call them) like shit. He pooh-poohed their theories, corrected their interpretations of his work and complained about everything — the minivan they hired to drive him about, his itinerary, the number and caliber of graduate students scheduled to attend the talk he was to give. But it all made sense when they were finally loading him back aboard the van. The griping, the dissatisfaction, the surliness were the very things that commanded respect. Dave was a patsy, he was too accommodating, too apologetic to ever enjoy anyone's respect. If there was ever a problem, Dave was always quick to take the blame. It was that way at Fisheries; he was always there to clean up someone else's mess. Dave needed to mend but he also needed to change.

Bet had been furiously cleaning the kitchen during Speidel's reception, but it was still a mess when the party ended. It was two-thirty in the morning when Alice, almost asleep on her feet, volunteered to take the Skoda and drive poor Bet, God-sent Bet, back home to Push Through. Dave suggested, and Alice agreed, that she should go straight home from there. Dave was cutting it close, and he didn't want to meet Alice in front of Phonse's shed. It would be altogether too suspicious.

He was going to make it clear to Phonse tonight that he could not become further involved with the R.S.V. prototype scheme. He would help him out this one night only. It might prove the end of their relationship, but it was all Dave could do. He would give Phonse the news once they had concluded whatever weird business his neighbor had planned for this sticky night.

The heat hadn't diminished and Dave's clothes were clammy as he headed to the cellar to steel himself for the trouble ahead. Just one last night, he thought.

12

Dave realized why Phonse had picked this night. Clouds had moved in, the sky thick with the day's heat. It was moonless, dark enough to hide his actions from the ever-watchful Winnebagos. Dave decided against carrying a flashlight, assuming that he could easily pick his way through the familiar woods. But in the pitch dark of the country night he realized that there were not simply one or two main trails between the restaurant and Phonse's property but an elaborate network, a spider's web of rabbit runs, all seeming to be, to the outstretched hand and a city boy's instinct, *the* trail. The moist, warm air brought out the mosquitos and blackflies by the millions. Feeding to breed, the bugs were eating Dave alive. Their demented electric buzzing, the frenzied clatter of their armor as they filled his ears, compounded his confusion.

Dave couldn't even see his feet as they tested the peat floor, spongy and full of pitfalls. Twice his glasses were plucked off his face by spruce branches and he had to grope for them among the moss and rot. After only a few steps he was lost. Stumbling around the woods until daylight would, however, provide Dave with an excuse for failing to rendezvous with Phonse, so he was at peace with his dilemma when, after twenty minutes, he collided with the back of Phonse's shed.

Dave was feeling his way along the side of the building when he felt the touch of cold metal, sensed the gun blue, against his neck.

"Phonse?" It was more a prayer than a question.

"Dave? Fuck, old man, you gave me a start." Phonse was whispering.

Dave wanted to scream at Phonse, wanted to put an end to all the foolishness, the nonsense, the moronic game, a game that had almost put a bullet in his throat, but his attention was focused on his bowels. Once again he had narrowly avoided shitting in his pants.

Phonse took Dave by the arm, led him round the big shed and through the door.

"Good thinking, Dave, coming around the back like that. I saw the Skoda coming down the drive and I'm trying to figure why you brought the car and then I sees Alice get out. Jesus, old man, I didn't have a clue what was up."

Dave had to sit. He was slightly nauseated and hung his head between his knees. Phonse wasn't concerned.

"You didn't see anybody around, did you, Dave?"

"No, Phonse." Dave decided not to mention the Cortini table. Phonse was, after all, armed and skittish.

"That doesn't mean they're not out there, you know, Dave. These people are professionals. I'm always more worried when things seem fine."

Dave looked up. He hadn't been in Phonse's shed since the night they hatched the rare-bird hoax. The R.S.V. was now free of its cables and balanced atop a spindly metal trolley fitted with giant cart wheels. The assembly, which was at least twelve feet high, was an odd mix of the modern and medieval, like a battering ram armed with a missile. It was far too top-heavy to even consider moving; Dave was worried that it might topple any second.

"What are you going to do with that?"

Phonse looked surprised that Dave would even ask. "Sea trials. We're going to take her down to the water."

Dave shook his head. "You're cracked, Phonse, if you think that's going to make it down to the water. How much does the damn submarine weigh?"

"She weighs twelve hundred pounds."

Dave couldn't assess whether this was accurate, or even whether twelve hundred pounds was heavy or light for a Recreational Submarine Vehicle.

"Ultra-lightweight Dave, that's key to the system. Now once she's full of ballast I would imagine . . . Anyway, that part is more complicated, you got to consider buoyancy. First calculations I made, I forget that it was salt water we were talking about. That would have been a disaster, would never have been able to get her to dive. She would have just floated."

Staring at the ludicrous metal cigar, Dave thought that getting the thing to sink was the least of Phonse's worries.

"What are you going to tow it with?" Dave knew the R.S.V. would never leave the shed. The question was academic.

"Tow? What? Take her over the roads? That would never do. If the crowd on the Upper Road saw this going by . . . " It was too preposterous to think about. Phonse's faith in the R.S.V. was so firm that he seriously considered someone might be interested in stealing it. "They would cut the moorings, set her adrift, then claim her as salvage."

"Phonse, if you're not going to tow it . . .?"

"We're going to wheel it down over the hill. I know it's a little rough. That's why the wheels are so big."

Again Dave couldn't see Phonse's reasoning.

"And that's where you come in, Dave," Phonse continued. "You're the brake man."

Dave laughed. "I have to say it, Phonse. You're after going off the deep end. I don't think that thing is stable enough to move anywhere, least of all over a cart trail, and in the pitch black. Besides all that, I'm not sure I want to be party to you drowning yourself."

Phonse frowned.

Dave retreated a little. "If anybody was to build one of these things, if I ever needed someone to make me a submarine, it would be you, naturally, but how do you know that this Uri guy, this Svetkov character, wasn't a kook?"

Phonse walked to Dave and put his arms around his shoulders. "Dave, my man, it comes as no surprise that you have doubts about the R.S.V. project. You think I'm some kind of lunatic bayman. Naturally, with all your education up on the mainland, you would be inclined to think that.

"But I can assure you I do not take this matter lightly. I have made the appropriate calculations." Phonse adopted a professorial tone. "I have run tests. Through certain channels, that I cannot divulge, I have made inquiries into old Uri Svetkov's credentials. I'm not asking much. I think I have been a good neighbor. I need your assistance this one night. After that you can forget you ever knew me, you can say, 'Alphonse Murphy? Who the fuck is he?' But, Dave, you are the only person I can trust at this time."

Everything he said was true. To further pressure Dave, Phonse added, "Any movement on the cocaine?"

The only movement on the cocaine had been straight up Dave's nose. And he had alienated Larry Doyle, the only person who might know where to sell it.

"No movement, not yet, though I might have a lead." After this lie Dave had to assist his neighbor.

"A lead. Good." Phonse was waiting for Dave to elaborate.

"Okay, Phonse. I'll help you."

Phonse smiled. "A drink, then, sort of like a christening."

Dave followed him to the barrels that served as a bar. Laid out, as it had been the last time, was a sample of the cocaine.

"Help yourself, Dave."

It was a test. If Dave partook, then Phonse would know that he had consumed most of the sample bag, that he had not made any inquiries. But Phonse probably knew already. Dave got a five-dollar bill from his wallet as Phonse poured up two tall rums.

As he was sipping the booze, Dave noticed that the floor around them was littered with dry, white animal bones, from a caribou perhaps. He had been idly kicking at them. "What's all this?"

"Bones. I was going to age them, extremes of heat and pressure to accelerate the process, then bury them. Dinosaurs. If the bird story worked, I figured why not?. But then I realized . . ." Phonse took a drink.

Dave was happy to hear that Phonse had abandoned this new scheme. "What changed your mind?"

"I read where they figure now that dinosaurs were more akin to birds, with hollows in the bone. Amazing coincidence, what? We got birds on the brain out here. Once I fabricates the right bird bones I'll be right back on track. The place will be covered with archaeologists. There will be a question of rights, then royalties . . ."

There was no stopping Phonse. Where Dave was paralyzed with indecision over the most trivial matter, Phonse stormed ahead, making a submarine that would probably serve as his coffin, now fashioning counterfeit dinosaur bones. What would Phonse do if the bones proved profitable? If paleontologists were as easily taken as ornithologists? Dave couldn't imagine Phonse retiring to sunnier climes with his booty. The man certainly couldn't stand being idle. It was all in the caper.

Phonse set down his drink. "I got a present for you, Dave. I was going to give it to you later but . . ." Phonse was, without saying it outright, admitting for the first time that the R.S.V. had risks, that he might not have another opportunity to give Dave the gift. He walked to a workbench, reached into an oil-stained cardboard box and pulled out an unpainted wooden hunting decoy. He brought it to Dave.

"Thanks, Phonse." Dave was grateful but puzzled. "It's a decoy."

"I made it myself."

Dave knew Phonse was an exemplary tinkerer, a wizard with an engine or motor, but the craftsmanship of the carving was breathtaking. The detail was miniature, the carved feathers had been worked with a tiny tool, painstakingly rendered so that the wooden surface had a velvety texture, it felt soft in the hand, downy like a bird, and Dave was compelled to treat it delicately. Likewise, the duck's bill had been carefully carved, sanded and pared so that it was unnervingly real to the touch. The eyes were sanded so smooth they shone. These eyes were the only failing in the sculpture. The eyes Phonse had crafted were alive, vital, they gave the duck a personality. This duck had charm.

"Phonse, it must have taken ages to —"

"It's no simple duck, Dave. That there is Tasker's sulphureous. The rarest of birds. I went back to the library, had a good study on it. I've got to paint it yet so you'll have to leave it with me. I figured it would be a nice decorative element in the dining room over at the Auk. The way I sees it, that bird has got to be good luck."

Dave had never been so touched by a gift, and if Alphonse Murphy felt that it would bring good luck, then it would. "Let's get this submarine in the water, Phonse," Dave said, his eyes growing watery.

The spidery wheeled contraption moved with more ease than Dave had thought possible. He was at the rear, pushing gently with his shoulder, all the while keeping a hand on the brake. The brake was simply a lever (originally an ax handle, he guessed) attached to a cable, which, through an elaborate system of pulleys, worked on the hubs of the two rear wheels. Phonse was to the front, within the contraption, behind the two front wheels. He steered by means of a metal bar that ran parallel to the front axle.

The first turn concerned Dave. They passed through the shed's big barn doors and veered toward the sea. The turn was quite gradual, yet the top-heavy weight began to swing and Dave could feel an upward momentum acting upon the wheel away from the turn. It wanted to capsize. If it did Dave would be able to jump free but Phonse, inside the matrix of pipes and bars, would be plucked up and catapulted into the woods. Dave hissed an alarm when he felt the machine lean, but Phonse gestured that everything was fine and for Dave to keep pushing. They had to be quiet so as not to wake Alice or Debbie. As they passed in front of the house, silently rolling over the dandelions and crabgrass, Dave looked over his shoulder at Alice's window and, for a moment, saw what could have been a silhouette. It was nerves, he was sure.

Phonse made Dave's responsibility clear — never, never ever, take his hand from the brake. The trail to the cove began just past the house. It was level at first. Only twice did a tree root or a small rut set the machine to swaying. As they approached the sea the trail began to slope slowly. Here Dave was to apply the brake to arrest the downward momentum. The last one hundred yards, heading toward the old rotting slipway, were another matter. There, the incline increased to almost forty-five degrees. Phonse calculated that at that point they would never be able to resist the pull, the stored potential energy, of the twelve hundred pounds straining toward the sea. They would stop at the crest of this final hill, and attach the machine to a winch Phonse had concealed in a thicket of windswept alders to ease the R.S.V. into the waves.

Perspiring from effort, pushing the submarine's jury-rigged gurney, engaged in something purely physical, gave Dave a good feeling, of helping a neighbor, the kind of thing he liked to imagine one did in the country. The R.S.V. didn't seem like more mischief but a serious project. Launching it was good work that had to be done.

The first, gentle slope began just where the light from Phonse's house ceased to penetrate the nocturnal gloom. Dave's pulse quickened. They were beginning to roll blindly into the night. Mosquitos were now nesting in Dave's ears, their deranged buzzing blocking the sound of the surf, but he could not take his hand from the brake to brush them away. He was applying his full strength to the lever and still the machine was slowly accelerating, the increasing speed amplifying the side-to-side swaying of its upper reaches.

"Phonse, it's getting away."

Phonse's answer was lost in the buzzing of the bugs. Dave tried digging his heels into the trail but the force of the machine's weight dragged his feet through the hard-packed peat-like plows.

As the velocity increased, the stress on the brake lever grew. Dave's forearm was becoming hot and hard with the strain. He felt his muscles cramping but dared not let go. The machine caught a rut and bounced, lifting his feet off the ground. Dave, legs splayed, was being dragged behind the juggernaut. Phonse shouted something — instructions? an alarm? He couldn't make it out. The machine was still accelerating. It bounced again, miraculously putting Dave back on his feet. But he was now running to keep pace with the big cart. The right rear wheel rose up as the machine listed to the left. Dave could hear the canvas straps that cradled the little submarine whining against the pressure as the metal cigar jumped and shimmied. There was suddenly a wild clattering, like a spinning raffle wheel. The spokes were eating through foliage. He could smell alder. They were leaving the trail, crashing into the bushes, passing the winch! The ground dropped away. They had lost all control of the rolling vehicle. Dave heard Phonse scream something, but it was laughter, not panic, in the raised voice. The machine was falling over itself, the heavy top end leaning forward over the wheelbase as it raced madly downhill. Dave heard pipes ringing as they sheared from the strain, metal rattling off metal. He felt the brake lever leaving his grasp. He was briefly airborne, his stomach turning over, unable to sense the direction of the ground, out of touch with gravity. His face collided with round beach rocks as the R.S.V., the machine carrying it and likely Phonse splashed loudly into the sea.

Dave thought his face would surely be a purple mess as he stood looking for the slipway. He could barely make it out a good thirty feet to his right. The cove looked oily under the black air, without a true surface, nothing more than a luminous presence. He staggered down to the water, the beach rocks shifting under his feet. He could smell the salt water and hear a gentle swell pulling the beach, the stones chattering. Was Phonse drowning? Dave stepped into the surf.

"Phonse?"

"Dave, old man. Are you okay?" The voice was coming from the water. Dave could hear him splashing.

"Phonse." Without thinking, Dave walked into the water, threw himself in to swim to Phonse's rescue. An involuntary gasp came from deep inside him. With the air so warm he did not expect to find the water frigid. As he swam farther out the water had its way with him, stronger than his best strokes.

"Phonse?" he shouted.

A wave picked him up, lifted him skyward. Where was the beach?

"Dave!"

Phonse was close. Dave swam toward his voice. He could see him now, see his thrashing arms. The swell dropped him, water rushed into his nose, the salt burning his throat. He was going to drown, he was going to die. His face ached. He had no strength in his arms, his clothes were constricting his movements, weighing him under.

"Dave!" The voice came from above. Phonse was high up above the surf, floating somehow. Dave's head collided with something hard. He felt his skull ring.

"Dave, old man." Fingers dug into his biceps. His arm was being yanked with cruel force. He was swinging, coming out of the water. His nose smashed against a wall, blood was running down his throat, mingling with the brine. There was a tug at his belt, his pants forced up between his buttocks. The water was falling away, his stomach was across something firm. He felt cold metal with his hands. His legs were no longer thrashing.

"Dave, old man, are you all right? What the fuck were you doing?"

Dave pushed himself up, and rested on his knees. Phonse was standing in front of him. They were on top of the R.S.V. It had evidently been catapulted into the ocean.

"Phonse?"

"I told you to stay back, Dave."

"I thought you were drowning." The submarine was moving beneath them, rolling slightly with the waves. Dave saw that only a small portion of the R.S.V. was above the water, that the area available to them as a floating island was very slight.

"Very fucking dangerous, Dave. I'm sorry. Very fucking dangerous. It's a miracle she was thrown into the water."

Dave turned carefully. He didn't want to be back in the cold ocean, ever. There was more light out here, more reflection back off the sea. The hill and the beach were difficult to make out, he couldn't really see them. He could only mark the end of the cove's reflective surface and sense the flat blackness beyond. The distant sound of the beach rocks shifting under the waves was a better measure.

"Phonse, we're drifting."

"Nice, what, she feels quite stable." Phonse bounced on his heels to demonstrate. The hollow vessel responded like a tin drum.

This wasn't nice. The sea was getting choppier, the swells deeper as they moved away from the land. They were already too far from the beach to attempt swimming back.

"What are we supposed to do? Do you have a life raft?"

"I've got a punt hidden on the other side of the cove. That's where I'm going to moor her."

"How in the name of God are we going to get over there?"

"In the R.S.V., Dave."

Phonse was speaking in a matter-of-fact tone. They were drifting out to sea on top of a homemade submarine, they had both almost drowned and come very close to being crushed by twelve hundred pounds of bad ideas. Dave was enraged.

"Fuck you, Phonse! *Fuck you!* I'm not getting in the goddamn submarine. You almost killed us. You don't know what the fuck is going on. Just look at what happened. What about your cockamamie cocksucking calculations?"

"I told you I was sorry. And I know what went wrong. I failed to consider the fuel."

"You what?"

"The fuel in the tank. Not the extra load, I considered that, but where it was sloshing around. That's why she was swinging and once we got to the last stretch . . . well, you felt her going yourself. It's a wonder she didn't blow up."

"Blow up." Dave's anger had quickly subsided. They were in a horrible predicament! And his nose was likely broken from having slammed into the R.S.V.

"I never wanted to force you into this, but we've got to get inside. There's nothing else for it, Dave. That's just the way it is."

It was all just the way it is. The world was just the way it was. The Auk was just the way it was, Claire was coming up to visit. Just like that. His nose was broken, his face was pulverized, he was slowly poisoning himself down in his cellar. Just that. Dave had to get in the submarine, after having just survived drowning, only to attempt it once more under the care of a lunatic with whom he had become inexorably entangled. Just that. It was lamentable coincidence at work, it was the force that killed his mother, the force that she acknowledged in death with that sorry salute to the fates, "Oh my, what can you do?"

Phonse must have sensed Dave's resignation, for the old guy was already squeezing down the tube that led inside the metal cigar. "It's a bit of squeeze, Dave, and mind the periscope."

It was more than a squeeze, it was too small for Dave. His legs were dangling inside the R.S.V. but any further passage was restricted by his gut, which hung over the lip of the tube — an airtight blubber cork. They would just have to float there all night, thought Dave. God willing, the coast guard would spot them and take them for smugglers. They would search Phonse's shed and the Auk, confirming their suspicion that drugs were involved and Dave would go to jail for years. At least he would get some rest in the big house. And he resolved that he would become a witness for the Crown on one condition: that he be sentenced to serve his term in any prison other than the one holding Phonse.

The sea was growing rougher, affected by the ground swells. They were leaving the shoals, coming to deeper waters. The bow of the R.S.V. was now pitching into the waves. Dave watched a curtain of icy water rise over the front of the submarine. Feeling the bone-numbing chill of the spray, he decided prison could wait. In a pathetic display of wriggling and squirming, he forced himself inside, a plump sausage emerging from a mill. He landed heavily on his hands and knees and heard Phonse slam something shut. A spinning wheel whined, a seal closed with a tight pucker.

Why had Dave imagined that one would be able to stand up in the R.S.V.? He had examined it hanging in the shed and should have reasoned that you would be confined to your hands and knees. Dave's busted-up face was hovering just behind Phonse's arse. Phonse read his mind.

"It's a prototype, Dave. The comfort will come, trust me."

Dave could see the weave of the fabric in the seat of Phonse's sopping trousers, he could see water squeezing between each bound fiber. The metal of the cigar, so smooth on the outside, was here scarred with an intricate tattoo of pocks and fissures. It was the magic lanterns again, the Svetkov lamps. Yes, Phonse had said they drew very little power.

The confinement and discomfort were joined by a staleness in the air. The little cigar was steaming up with the moisture from their clothes. It was hard to breathe. Dave mentioned this.

"That's because there's no oxygen," said Phonse.

Suffocation would also pre-empt incarceration.

"It's a good sign, Dave. It proves she's tight." At least holding your breath you wouldn't have to sniff at the rear end of the captain.

"Once I start her up the pumps will kick in. There will be oxygen enough for all hands. Then we'll be off."

He was completely at the mercy of Phonse and his machine, on his hands and knees, trapped. This was a hazing, another step in a rough amateur brainwashing. All the elements were in place: the drugs, the sleep deprivation, the shared secrets. The R.S.V. would surface miles from Push Cove at Phonse's island headquarters where Dave would join the bayman's unholy army of zombies. A quick accounting of his surroundings only made Dave feel more desperate. Where the outside of the R.S.V. had a finished look, the inside of the submarine looked like the guts of Phonse's snowblower, all exposed pipes and hoses and valves. An unknown fluid was dripping slippery on his neck.

"Now," Phonse was speaking to himself, "I believe this one is the fuel."

Dave saw that none of the valves were labeled. Nor were the gauges Phonse was studying. Dave was sure that even the most highly trained submariner relied on labels. The military taught you how to put a rifle together in the dark, but the advanced operations, the jet jockeying, the targeting of missiles and surely the navigation of submarines required more than intuition and feel.

"Fucking Svetkov lamps," Phonse grumbled. Dave craned his neck to look over Phonse's buttocks at the controls. He tried to make out the numbers and symbols on the gauges but, just as Phonse had said they would, the figures seemed to be floating several inches in front of the displays. Dave closed his eyes and shook his head. He looked back at the dials. The digits were still floating, the circle of numbers was unraveling, impossible to comprehend.

Phonse flicked a switch and Dave felt the vibrations run up his arms and legs, set his flab to jiggling. They were not atop an engine but in its midst. Phonse looked back over his shoulder at Dave. His smile was angelic. This was heaven for the crazy bayman, inside his own machine, part of it.

"Dave." Phonse paused dramatically. "Run silent. Run deep."

Phonse pushed a lever and pulled at a knob. Did the R.S.V. have a standard transmission? Dave wondered. Had Phonse adapted an old Vauxhall engine for submersible operation? The R.S.V. lurched and they were off.

As Phonse promised, the pumps kicked in with a belch to deliver oxygen. It was thickly mixed with fumes. Dave could taste the fuel.

"It works, Dave! It works!" Dave could tell that Phonse had not been certain until this very moment that the R.S.V. would function. Now that the contraption worked, Dave felt they should quickly get to the stashed punt. There was nothing more to prove except that one could merely survive. But how did you steer a submarine? You didn't look out a window. Fuck, thought Dave, we are under water.

"Are we under water Phonse?"

"Guess what, Dave?"

Dave was afraid to know.

"Dive, dive, dive!" Phonse shouted. The front of the R.S.V. dipped. Dave slid forward, his tender nose coming hard up against Phonse's rear end.

"Excuse me, Phonse." Why was he apologizing?

Phonse was giggling, a child happy with a silly toy. Dive? Dave remembered they always said that on *Voyage to the Bottom of the Sea*. Richard Basehart? Who was the other guy on the show? *The Bottom of the Sea*? "Full fathom five, thy father . . ."

"Phonse, how do you know where you're going?"

"Sonar, Dave, sonar." Phonse tapped on a small screen to his left. It displayed a series of incomprehensible squiggles over a background of video noise, like a television tuned between channels. Even under the Svetkov lamps Dave could tell a forty-dollar fish finder was their only guide home.

"Twelve fathoms," said Phonse. "Thirteen fathoms. Is that thirteen? No, it's seventeen. Seventeen fathoms, Dave!"

The thought had occurred to Dave before, usually during a rough approach and landing at St. John's airport after drinking too much on the flight, "I am now ready to die. I have seen this moment before, I was born with it, I am intimate with every microsecond as it elapses. This is my death."

"Eighteen fathoms!" To die never having made love to Alice . . . He did love her, he thought, his raw lust had tempered. He needed to be with her, needed to hear her voice as much as he craved her touch.

"Twenty-four fathoms. No, it's twelve! No, that can't be right."

How could he think of Alice at a time like this? What of Claire? Didn't his commitment to her mean anything? Weren't people supposed to work on relationships? The failure of their marriage was not tragic but trite. The union had not crashed calamitously but had grown derelict from neglect. Though he knew it to be as self-serving as a deathbed confession, he vowed to make an effort.

"Thirty fathoms? It must be thirty. These goddamn lights are a torment."

Dave watched Phonse rap the gauge with his knuckles, trying to coax some sense out of it. But reconciliation with Claire, he realized, was simply retreat. While the workload at the Auk was breaking him, he was having fun too. He was doing what he wanted. Dave was an artist, however minor, in the kitchen. In orchestrating his nightly celebration he was occasionally creating sublime moments for people. Would throwing that away be courageous? Wasn't his fear of moral judgment for having blown his marriage the ultimate cowardice?

What was the alternative to the Auk? Going back to Fisheries, overseeing the dismantling of the way of life that had defined Newfoundland for four centuries and coming home every day to the yet harder job of being an adequate husband?

A tiny, sharp *ping* filled the sub. Phonse was suddenly very still, holding his breath.

"What is it, Phonse?"

"Thirty-two fathoms may well be the upper limit of the hull's pressure tolerance there, Dave."

The sound came again. A perfect, precise tone. *Ping*. Death at the door.

"I'll just ease her up, Dave."

The submarine leveled off for a moment before slowly ascending.

"Congratulations, Captain Murphy." Dave didn't feel like commending Phonse but thought he should humor him in an effort to hasten their return to shore.

"Thank you, Dave. It's incredible, isn't it. One last maneuver and we're out of here."

How could Dave argue? He wasn't about to seize the controls.

After five minutes of motion Dave had lost all sense of direction. Phonse, trying hopelessly to consult charts encrypted by the Svetkov beams, still claimed to have matters well in hand. Cramping up, Dave rolled over and lay on his back. For some reason looking at the ceiling of the tubular container made him feel more claustrophobic than had looking at Phonse's arse. It was soon time to beg.

"Please, Phonse, I'm having an anxiety attack, I have to get out."

"Not uncommon, Dave, not uncommon at all. I read where they put prospective submariners through an incredible battery of psychological tests. Last thing you want is someone cracking up in a submarine."

"But, Phonse, that's what I'm saying, I'm cracking up."

"No, I mean like a full-fledged nut-out Dave, you know, screaming and yelling 'Let me out, let me out.'"

Phonse had effectively taken from Dave the option of screaming those very words.

"This is where it may get interesting, Dave. Up periscope!"

The periscope didn't actually go up. In fact, it sort of came down. Phonse told Dave to pull at a greased post above him. Doing so revealed yet another instrument of Phonse's design. It was simply an old telescope tube inside a lubricated metal pipe. Dave got back on his hands and knees and put his eye to a viewer that appeared to have been recovered from a pair of binoculars. Dave thought of the birders. With his glasses on, it took him a second to focus through the diopter, but when he did he forgot his fears for the first time since entering the water. There, plain as day, was the community wharf at Push Through. He could see the long-liners, tied up since the fish had been exterminated, bobbing somnolently at their moorings. He could see beyond, into the tiny town. He saw poor Bet's house.

"It's amazing, Phonse."

"It's Push Through, I hope."

"Large as life."

"Anything stirring? Don't want anyone to notice the smoke."

Of course, the exhaust would come to the surface. Dave turned the pipe. The rotation was a disappointing thirty or forty degrees. He saw something.

"Yes!"

"What?"

"There's a car out on the wharf, couple of guys standing round it."

"We had better move off, Dave, that crowd will —"

"Shit, Phonse," Dave interrupted. "I've seen one of them. He was at the restaurant tonight. Guy named Cortini."

The suspicious diner was talking to one of his lackeys, lecturing the man, gesticulating angrily, saying much more in a few seconds on the Push Through community wharf at four o'clock in the morning than he had all night at the restaurant.

As Phonse turned the R.S.V., Cortini and his man left the scope's frame. Push Through, its lights twinkling, rolled by, then the bald hills surrounding the town, then nothing but black night.

Cortini! There was something peculiar about the guy. Alice had noticed it right away.

"They must be the smugglers, Phonse." Back for their missing bale of blow.

"Dave, think about it. Smugglers having got away with it don't come back looking for a stray bale. The man is obviously with the goddamn Winnebago Corporation. Industry is the new frontier of espionage, Dave. Uri told me so. You've got all these spooks out there with nothing to do. There will always be trouble. The Communists gone, what odds we'll turn the Barbie Doll corporation into the new enemy? Not to suggest anything untoward about Barbie now, Dave, but you got to see my point."

Dave supposed it was possible. They were, after all, traveling beneath the surface of Push Cove, an idea he had dismissed as another of Phonse's delusions only an hour earlier. Dave had imagined that Uri Svetkov was just another crackpot who found a willing audience for his theories in Alphonse Murphy, yet now it was evident that the Bulgarian's plans for a miniature submarine were genuine. But if Dave came to believe in the existence of agents from the Winnebago Corporation lurking in the woods around the Auk, he would have to accept so much more, all the crackpot conspiracy theories would have credence, he would become a member of the Cult of Risk, the Cult of Phonse. He would become a believer, obediently studying the sacred text of happenstance.

"I'm going to open her up, Dave. Get home before daylight." Phonse pushed the throttle down hard, forcing the engines to a growl and Dave's kidneys to quivering.

Phonse had built a discreet, rudimentary dock for the R.S.V. in a small cave on the far side of Push Cove. The cliffs here were too steep to have allowed settlement and the area remained wild. The only people ever visiting the barrens above the cave were occasional berry pickers and rabbit hunters in the fall of the year.

The R.S.V.'s hidden bay could only be detected from the water, and then only by someone looking for it. The ceiling of the cave was not high and the sluicing wave action within its confines was irregular, choppy. As Dave was emerging from the R.S.V., the water in the cave rose quickly, lifted the submarine, and his head was dashed against the rocks above. Another scar for his collection.

Dave and Phonse were quickly in the punt motoring across Push Cove. Dave was bruised through. There were lumps on his head, and to the touch his nose seemed swollen to twice its normal size, though thankfully unbroken. His muscles were sore from swimming in his clothes and cramped from having crouched in the R.S.V. for an hour and a half. Still, he found the early dawn beautiful. The water had calmed. The sun was not yet over the horizon but the sky was already filling with light. A vermilion band was forming at the horizon, sunrise emerging warm from the deep blue. Red sky at morning, sailors take warning. The putter of the tiny outboard motor was a comfort. It wasn't appropriate to speak; words would only poison the perfect air. And, after the previous night, what was to be said? Farther up the small bay the lights of Push Through were still visible in the half-light. The roofs of Phonse's house and the Auk could be seen peeking out of the stunted spruce on the hills opposite.

Fatigue permeated Dave's every fiber but he felt he had really done something, been part of a great accomplishment.

They put ashore at the old slipway. Phonse stayed behind to clear up traces of the R.S.V. launch, insisting that Dave get back to the Auk and rest.

Dave's legs were heavy as he climbed the hill. He wouldn't remember crawling into his bed, sliding beneath the sheets and falling into a chasm of deep sleep.

13

Dave surfaced at one-thirty in the afternoon. Alice and Bet had handled lunch again. For the first time in months Dave felt rested. He hadn't slept so late in years. Stepping from the bed, he felt stiff but not seriously damaged. He felt athletic. He gingerly touched his nose. It still felt a little swollen. He went to the bathroom mirror to take a full inventory of his injuries.

The face had suffered no cuts or abrasions from its impact with the beach. The nose looked fine. The only problem was the eyes, both of them blackened. His collision with the R.S.V. while swimming to Phonse's rescue had resulted in two shiners, mirror-image purple crescents under each eye. Dave thought the bruises made him appear kind of tough, but he certainly didn't look forward to concocting an explanation. Almost any other mark on the body could be dismissed as the result of clumsiness, having tripped, fallen down a few stairs, but black eyes always read boozing, violence, trouble.

Dave searched for his sunglasses. He had purchased a pair of prescription shades years ago, before he and Claire had gone on their Caribbean honeymoon. He hadn't found much use for them during the holiday since they had spent most of the two weeks happily in bed.

Digging through the drawers, he turned up a bathing suit of Claire's, panties, ankle socks, a pair of tights snaking through a brassiere — the bones of their relationship, heaved to the surface by a deep, hard frost of love lost.

Dave wasn't the type of man to wear sunglasses. He thought them an affectation in Newfoundland. He finally found some among swimming trunks and T-shirts that would now make a pudding of him. (More relics, more solemn ticks of the clock.) The glasses were dated, big teardrop aviator models. He put them on and peered at himself. He looked as though he had crawled out of 1978.

Thankfully the sun was shining as hot and pointy as it ever did in Newfoundland. The kitchen was sizzling from the high, white midday light coming through the windows.

Bet didn't seem to notice anything unusual about Dave's appearance, but Alice shot him a bemused glance when she entered from the dining room.

"Afternoon, Dave."

Dave guessed that she didn't want to make him self-conscious by asking about the disco shades.

"You two are saints. Have I ever told you that?"

"Thank you, Dave." Alice was grinning. "And no, you haven't."

"I appreciate you letting me sleep. I was bagged."

"You looked terrible yesterday. I thought you were coming down with something."

"So did I. But today I feel like a million bucks."

"I've just got the one table left to set." Alice departed for the dining room.

Dave pulled a stool up to the counter by the window to bathe in the heat. A tremendous weight had been lifted from him. He was square with Phonse.

He watched Bet working, vigorously scrubbing pots. Since she had returned to the Auk, Bet was better dressed, more confident. It was Alice's influence; she never talked down to Bet but treated her as an equal. Dave realized, after watching the two of them relate, that he always addressed Bet in a slightly raised voice, as if being a touch simple meant she was also hard of hearing. He stopped doing so.

"Long day yesterday, Bet."

"It was a long day, Mr. Purcell." Bet smiled. She always seemed to find something amusing about idle chitchat. "The crippled man is back now. He was in the parking lot with his friends."

"The crippled man?"

"The man from last night. With his friends. They're down by the water."

Alice entered the kitchen.

"So Herr Dr. Speidel has returned." Dave gave a fascist salute. Alice didn't appreciate the joke.

"And Mr. Cortini," Alice added. "Cortini was talking to Speidel in the parking lot before the crowd went off in search of the famous duck."

What was this? What would people from Winnebago want with Speidel?

"Cortini. I saw him last night!"

Alice stopped in her tracks. "What? After he left?"

Dave realized he had let the cat out of the bag. "No. Here. At the restaurant."

Alice shook her head, impressed by Dave's stupidity. Dave continued.

"What were they talking about?"

Alice got herself a Heineken and sat next to Dave at the counter. It wasn't like her to have a beer so early in the day. She drank from the green bottle and looked out at the spruce woods. "I wouldn't be able to tell what they were saying, would I, Dave." Dave realized this was true. "But this Cortini guy, I didn't like him, his table left exactly fifteen percent as a tip last night, down to the penny. That just drives me nuts. What a way to live your life, continually calculating. Anyway, this morning he comes up to Speidel in the parking lot and makes the old guy very upset. He wasn't yelling at him or anything, but leaning over him, speaking very carefully, you know. Speidel seemed angry first and then kind of sheepish."

"Well, you know these bird people. They can be very . . . strange." Dave wasn't about to repeat Phonse's sentiments that merciless agents from a recreational-vehicle giant were probably now playing their cruel hand.

"Some kind of shades you got there, Dave. Planning on going cruising in the Skoda?"

The gentle mockery took Dave below the belt; he felt like an awkward teenager. He had a crush on her. "It's bright."

"It's a look," said Alice, "for sure, it's a look."

"I'm going to check out the Speidel crowd. They didn't come in to eat?"

"Didn't you see them, Dave? Last night was this decade's extravagance. They're box lunch types, cheese sandwiches, little bottles of tomato juice and binoculars."

Dave got off the stool and marched outside into the heat of the sun.

Dave's footfalls threw up a little dust as he walked the trail to the sea. He would investigate these queer goings-on, find the connection between Speidel and Cortini before alerting Phonse. Dave hoped, with the R.S.V. launched and hidden across the bay, that Phonse's concerns about security would relax. There was no sense in sounding an alarm until there was real trouble.

Dave imagined the Speidel group would be spread along the coast, casting a wide net for the ghost duck, but when he reached the cliffs directly behind the Auk he saw them clustered around Speidel by the old slipway. He worried that there might still be evidence of the previous evening's shenanigans on the beach, and hurried toward them.

There was consternation in the group. There was much shaking of heads, frowns, kicking at stones. Dave recognized the enthusiastic man who had spoken to him at the late-night buffet, now glum.

"What's up?" Dave said, forcing a grin. Dave was bad at faking a smile, he looked like the Joker from the

Batman comics. What a caper! Fuck-Up Man impersonating the Joker.

"It's just terrible. Terrible," said the man. Dave looked at the others. Whatever it was, there was a consensus that it was indeed terrible.

"What's terrible?" Dave had almost added "this time?" The demeanor of the academics reminded him of the crowd at Fisheries. At Fisheries they were always concerned, always reacting first with panic and then with resignation to ever more bad news. They could never get used to it. Dave felt above that now. He had traveled under the waters of Push Cove in an R.S.V. prototype, had risked his life. Dave was a man of action.

"Will these Newfs never learn?" said the man. "I know I shouldn't say it, but they truly are barbarians. They've killed off the fish but they won't stop there, will they?"

Dave was a Newf so didn't quite know how to respond. He resisted the impulse to apologize. Besides, he wasn't sure what Newfoundland had done this time. "What have we killed off now?"

"Perhaps nothing yet, but look. *Look!*" The man pointed to the beach. The rocks were shiny, reflecting sickly rainbow tones. The beach was stained with oil, no doubt from the R.S.V. launch.

"It's not the Exxon *Valdez*." Dave knew this was the wrong response. The man glowered at him. It was just the thing he expected to hear from someone whose progenitors had murdered an entire race of people.

"My good man." His tone was patronizing. "There are probably very few Tasker's sulphureous, perhaps only a single mating pair, and there is certainly enough oil on this beach to destroy one of them."

There may have been enough oil, only there were no Tasker's sulphureous to destroy, just a big fat lie.

"I fear we may be alarmed without reason, gentlemen." It was Speidel. Dave imagined the group rolling the huge man down the hill. Considering the troubles he and Phonse had encountered with the R.S.V. it couldn't have been easy. At least the big Bavarian hadn't ended up in the drink. "I actually doubt whether we will find the bird here."

The crowd murmured. Though it wasn't his place, Dave piped up.

"Too hot for a duck, is it, Professor?"

Everybody turned and stared. Who was this bayman bold enough to question the great learned German? Speidel turned his chair, wheels slipping and sliding over the smooth beach rocks, to face Dave.

"No, my friend. It is not too hot for a duck. Tasker's sulphureous has been known to winter as far south as the Florida Everglades. No, the problem here is habitat. This is simply the wrong habitat for Tasker's sulphureous. They require a brackish marsh, a lagoon."

This was very serious. Word must not get out that the great Hans Speidel, the foremost advocate for the extinct duck, was dismissing the Push Cove sighting.

"But . . . but someone saw it here," Dave said.

Speidel was indicating that he wished to leave, to be wheeled up the hill, away from Dave's inanities.

"Didn't they?" Dave addressed the question to the entire group. He was pleading. No one answered. They seemed to pity Dave. Where only moments earlier he had lived in the presence of the treasured duck, he was now just another silly bayman. He had fallen from grace. They started pushing Speidel up the hill.

Everyone was down in the mouth, a party had abruptly ended, and they had to go home early.

The man who had scolded Dave over the presence of the oil was talking, in hushed tones, to a colleague. "I can't remember any saltwater marsh near Fox Bite," he said as he passed Dave and joined the sad procession up the hill.

Dave sat on the beach. The caper was over almost as quickly as it had begun. He should have sold the Auk, got out when the going was good. Of course it had to end eventually, he couldn't have expected the birders to continue a fruitless search forever.

The sun was disappearing behind heavy clouds that were coming across the sky like a gray blanket. Push Cove had been pronounced dead. The temperature was dropping. A wind off the water chilled Dave. Red sky at morning, sailors take warning.

Dave came into the kitchen a sodden mess. Halfway up the trail the heavens had opened, dumping buckets of icy water on him. Alice's place at the counter had been taken by Phonse, who was eating a large plate of linguini in a tomato and salt cod sauce, another of his favorites from the Auk's menu. Bet must have served him.

"You got to like it, Dave." He nodded at his plate. "The Portageeze go in for this kind of thing."

"They figured it out, Phonse."

"What?" Phonse was alarmed.

"The duck. Speidel just said the habitat was all wrong."

"What does he know?"

"Everything, Phonse, he's one of the most respected ornithologists in the world. Besides, he's right. There is no duck, remember?"

"It's still only his opinion."

Phonse found it unacceptable that experts from abroad should come to Push Cove and make pompous pronouncements. They, the livyers — the original settlers — said the duck was there and that was that.

"It's a shame I didn't put the place on the market while we were doing such good business." He was thinking of Claire's impending arrival, how disappointed she would be having heard of the Auk's success and coming back to Newfoundland to find it empty, how she would hector him for yet another lapse in judgment.

"Dave, you're throwing in the towel again. This is by no means settled."

"I guess that's what he and Cortini were talking about."

"The guy on the wharf! Who was talking to him?"

"Speidel, this morning."

Phonse's brow furrowed. "That's a bit strange, don't you think, Dave? Why would the fucking Winnebagos stick their nose in the bird business?"

"No, Phonse! Cortini is obviously some bird guy, another expert. He's not with Winnebago."

"What is a bird watcher doing on the Push Cove wharf

at four o'clock in the morning, Dave? No. There's something strange about all this."

Phonse was again demonstrating his incredible propensity for understatement.

"I meant to talk to you about this Cortini fellow anyway, Dave. With the R.S.V. out of the shed I thought we could afford to take measure of the Winnebagos."

"Sure, Phonse." The more he thought about the situation, the more depressing it all seemed. With a decline in bookings he would have to let Alice go.

"Dave, old man, cheer up, it's not over yet. Plan B, Dave! Time to go to Plan B."

"I thought we already employed Plan B, Phonse."

"Dave! No problem, we move to Plan C." Phonse started to laugh, slapping Dave hard on the back. "Always have a Plan C!" With a napkin he wiped the corners of a saucy grin. "Run silent. Run deep!" he said.

At the kitchen door he laughed again, harder, his eyes watering.

Dave listened as the laughter disappeared into the woods.

14

Just three days after Speidel's decision that Push Cove was not the appropriate habitat for Tasker's sulphureous, the Auk had its first empty tables since May. People were canceling reservations they had placed weeks in advance.

In the days following, Dave had seen small groups of birders in the area, not peering through their heavy binoculars but standing around, hands in pocket, heads hung, commiserating with each other.

The news hadn't simply put off the birders but had given the place an aura of failure. Push Cove was home to disappointment, the place where something wonderful almost happened, but didn't. There was a story in the back pages of the St. John's daily with the headline "Duck Again Extinct."

Dave did not close up as planned. What was the point? He would have an extended, if not permanent, vacation soon enough.

It was obvious that his sour disposition put Alice off. She was aloof, not wanting to be dragged into his mire.

Now, at times idle, she shielded herself with yellowing paperbacks, secondhand numbers, British editions of James and Woolf and Lowry with print woven tight enough to deflect even the most concentrated rays of ennui. In the kitchen Dave grew careless with preparations and twice dishes were sent back.

Some of the few diners now at the Auk were twitchers from abroad on long-planned expeditions. They were surly, feeling cheated; the space reserved on their precious lists for Tasker's sulphureous would remain forever blank.

Things were coming unraveled quicker than Dave's most pessimistic estimates. Again he was uncorking his most treasured bottles to keep them from the receiver.

The only person rooting for the Auk was Minister of Tourism, Heber Turpin. Turpin called Dave in a funk. "It's an outrage, Mr. Purcell, an outrage! Goddamn foreign experts sticking their nose in it! They are a plague on Newfoundland, a plague! Christ sake, a fucking Kraut coming over here telling Newfoundlanders about our ducks. We'll get our own fucking experts on the case. I have friends down at Wildlife, Dave, I can send them around."

Remembering the effects of similar political pressures on the estimates of fish stocks when he was at Fisheries, Dave declined Turpin's offer.

The situation took a most bizarre turn ten days after Speidel's decision on the duck. Dave was unenthusiastically preparing lunch when a tremendous racket came from the dining room. He passed through the swinging doors to investigate and saw what he first thought to be an elderly gentleman having a heart attack. His burden of cameras, lenses and binoculars gave him away as a birder. He was gesturing madly and talking a blue streak.

A group of diners were forcing him into a chair, trying to calm him, when Dave asked Alice what was going on.

"He crashed through the door, he's been screaming about the duck."

The man was explaining himself to a table of attentive twitchers.

"As you can imagine, I was in quite a state. I thought it was just a greater sulphureous and then I looked through my binoculars and I saw the tuft on the head. I saw the tuft! It was very far off, near the other side of the bay. I went for my camera and I thought I'd lost it when I saw it again. I got one shot but when I went for another it was gone."

"You're very sure it had the swept-back tuft on the head?"

"It was a perfect specimen," the man replied, "perfect male specimen."

"Was there a female?"

"I didn't see one."

Alice brought the man a glass of brandy. He was having a hard time catching his breath. Dave could see he was a crazy — too long beating the bushes for grouse and chickadees. So now the cursed duck was akin to the Loch Ness monster, a hazy phantom that would appear every so often through the fog on Push Cove, dismissed as nonsense by serious ornithologists but forever championed by a loyal following of quacks. Dave supposed there was a sister restaurant to the Auk in Scotland, on the shores of that famous murky lake. The Auk could possibly survive by hawking trinkets and novelties, duck key chains and T-shirts, candy duck eggs and whatnot. Dave returned to the kitchen to overcook some halibut.

The next day he stopped at Dick's Service Station on the Upper Road to fill the Skoda's tank and buy some cigarettes. He couldn't remember having driven there. His mind was beginning to drift again, to leave the earth for the clouds.

Dick's son, Dick Junior, handed Dave his smokes and change. Dave read the pack of cigarettes. "Smoking Can Kill You," it said. How soon? wondered Dave.

"Duck's back," said Dick Junior.

"Oh, I think the fellow got it confused with some other duck."

Dave was determined not to let any light shine on his despair. Why set himself up for disappointment?

"No, b'y. He's picture's in da paper."

Dick Junior passed the newspaper to Dave. There it was, on page three, Tasker's sulphureous duck bobbing peacefully on the sea. The photo was out of focus but there was no mistaking the tell-tale tuft on its head. Nor was it hard to see why this bird caused such a fuss. It almost seemed to be smiling, it was so content. There was no doubt about it, this duck was a charm.

The tires of the Skoda screeched with pain as Dave pulled on to the Upper Road. He had urgent business with Alphonse Murphy.

"They'll just keep studying the photo until they notice something wrong, they'll blow up sections until they see some flaw." Dave was railing at Phonse in the shed. Phonse was up to his elbows in engine. Dave supposed a spaceship might be the next project.

"Who is going to blow up the photo, Dave? The international bird police? Inter-Bird?"

This was a good point.

"Everybody but you wants the duck to be out there, Dave. I don't understand it."

"I want it to be there, of course I do, but the *real thing*."

"That's not possible, is it, Dave? The bird is extinct. This is the next best thing."

"You are missing the point entirely, Phonse. The more elaborate you make the scam the easier it gets to screw up. It's a law of nature." Dave could tell Phonse wasn't worried. "How did you do it, anyway?"

"I just hooked that decoy I made for you onto the periscope and did a few sweeps of the bay. I took care to paint 'er just so. Right out of the book. I would dive every now and then so that no one could get too good a study on it. It's almost a mile from this shore. I'm surprised buddy got such a good picture. He must have the finest kind of gear."

"You've been out in the R.S.V. again, then?"

"Three missions. Working out the bugs."

"Do me a favor, will you, Phonse? Don't do it again."

"Not to worry, Dave, I lost the decoy. Must have got knocked off when I was docking her."

"Good, I'm glad."

"I'll bet you have a full house tonight."

"I dare say I will. Poor deluded bird brains."

Back at the Auk Dave felt bad for having given Phonse such a hard time. The man was only doing what he thought was best, and sure enough every table was booked. Dave saw some smiling birders quickly marching down to the shore. They were overjoyed, the bird thought dead and resurrected and dead again was back. Dave supposed the farce would never end. Phonse was right to laugh. If interest in the bird waned they could always turn to ersatz dinosaur bones.

Dave felt like celebrating. They had come back from the brink, seen their end and returned, a phoenix from the ashes. They were saved. Phonse's hand could hardly be called divine intervention but it was close. The great bird caper had taken yet another turn, twisted Möbius-like and come back on itself, and Dave was part of the show. The audience had taken their seats in the dining room and Dave was directing. Sauces tonight would be reduced just that much more, syrup to candy, incredibly rich. He asked Alice to put something a little jazzy on the stereo, excite the crowd. He danced with Bet, grabbed her by the arm and swung her to Art Tatum.

Alice tried, but failed, to suppress a big toothy smile when she came into the kitchen and discovered Dave and Bet desperately faking a tango.

"God bless that stupid duck," Alice had said.

And God bless Alphonse Murphy, thought Dave. This was the life. It was a night for flambé. Tenderloins of beef and pork got the brandy treatment, splashed slapdash in the skillet and, with an artful tilt of the pan, set afire. Dave tossed pastas high in the air, the sauces mingling with delicate noodles just so, never spilling a drop. He studied fish on the grill, listening with his perfect sizzle pitch for the ideal moment to flip them with gusto. He had a spoon in one hand, tongs in the other. He tossed shallots over his shoulder, they found the oil and rang like a cymbal.

The dining room was a festival. Every bite of salad sprayed crisp cool juices, tasting of green and sun and earth. The wines were rubies and topaz in the candlelight. Tables were talking to one another. Elbows hung over the backs of chairs. The air was jagged with laughter. It was the party to end all parties. The brilliant tone of a vibraphone buoyed Dave, let him float about the kitchen. Milt Jackson was cooking.

During her trips to the kitchen Alice was carelessly colliding with Dave, her hips banging into his, lingering a little. She put on a show of mock jealousy with Bet, wondering out loud why Bet got to dance with Dave and not her. Was she flirting? She was! She was!

The last of the orders prepared, Dave uncorked a magnum of 1982 Pichon Lalande, poured himself a big glass and walked into the dining room carrying the bottle. He was two steps past the door when he heard applause. There were some faces he had seen before and all a little drunk, the clapping a bit of a lark, but still it was touching. It was a triumph, however minor. However insignificant the Auk was, however far Dave's little place was from the legendary eateries of Paris or New York, this was one of the great nights to have dined.

He filled a few empty glasses with the luscious Pichon, talked a little small talk, talked a little wine, pled ignorance to all matters ornithological. He graciously shrugged off praise, saying it was a pleasure to serve, inviting patrons back.

Alice poured a few brandies for the stragglers, called two of the drunk ones expensive taxi rides back to St. John's. At two-thirty they were alone in the dining room. They were not inclined to speak, so worked, so dizzied were they by the rush and crush of the night that they bathed in the silence. Dave had plunked his arse in a chair at one of the empty tables. Alice was seated at the bar, studying a cognac. She flipped off her shoes as she did at the end of every evening.

"Come here," said Dave.

She smiled and sauntered to his table.

"Sit," said Dave. He heard his voice issue the invitation, a command with comic authority. Dave was acting impulsively, surprising himself.

Alice pulled out a chair and sat.

"Here." Dave gestured for her feet. She placed them across his knee. He took one of her feet in both hands and began kneading the soles. Alice let her head drop over the back of her chair and issued a contented sigh, a sigh of pleasure at Dave's touch.

He could feel the tension beneath the flesh of the perfect feet giving way beneath the hosiery. The air was redolent of Alice's musky perfume. A wave of heat, hot chocolate, wood stove warmth was filling Dave. This was where he wanted to be, here, now, with Alice. He wanted to crawl under the covers with her, spoon up against her back and her bum. There was a tug at his groin, an insistent push. He wanted to taste her, to get ahold of her, to have her legs wrapped round him, to slide inside her.

"Dave." She was almost whispering. "If we went on a date, where would you take me for dinner?"

Dave didn't know what to say.

"I hear the Auk is really quite wonderful," Alice said.

Dave laid her feet on the floor. Alice expectantly sat up in her chair. He was, he was going to kiss her, right now.

Bet came through the swinging doors, her fluorescent windbreaker zipped tightly to the top no matter what the weather, her silly little handbag clutched in both hands.

"I'm ready now, Alice," said poor Bet.

15

Dave woke feeling out of sorts. After showering and dressing, he found himself in the wine cellar. Having no idea what forces had carried him there, he quickly left. He was itchy. He should have been on top of the world, the caper was saved, he had cooked like a true master the night before and it now seemed certain that his feelings for Alice were reciprocated. Even so, his skin was crawling. His morning espresso tasted sour. And though his eyes were no longer blackened, he donned the stupid-looking aviator shades to block out the sun. Its rays seemed poisonous.

At his grocery wholesaler in St. John's Dave threw a tantrum over the state of the lettuce, shouting that he would be obliged to grow his own greens if matters did not improve.

He was speeding over the Upper Road blowing the Skoda's sad, squeaky horn at the car cannibals, hoping to piss them off. Phonse had strongly advised against aggravating these dangerous neighbors.

Crashing through the kitchen door with his supplies, he spewed oaths. "What kind of a fucking dump is St. John's? Is it asking too much to get a head of lettuce that hasn't turned brown! Are we on Baffin fucking Island? Do I look like Sir John fucking Franklin?" These were directed at no one in particular, it was a broad stroke, scattershot aimed at assholes at Fisheries, at the tweedy bird brains, at Claire's snotty friends. Only after deciding that it was imperative that he visit the cellar did Dave realize what was wrong.

He fetched a beer to settle his nerves and lit a cigarette. He had an addictive personality, coming from a long line of alcoholics, but then so did all of Newfoundland, a great westward wave of boozebags had sailed across the pond to settle the place.

This was not the day to concede defeat. Tonight he was planning on making love to Alice. The answer for it was a small dose, enough to put him on an even keel. It wouldn't do to be scratching at insects beneath his skin as he was trying to lure beautiful Alice into his bed. Yes, a small dose, he decided as Phonse came through the kitchen door.

"Dave!"

"Phonse, I'm a drug addict."

"Oh." Phonse was unconcerned. "I've got lots of drugs if that's the problem."

"No, Phonse, you see —"

"Power is out."

"I think I'm in love with Alice."

"Can't say I didn't warn you, Dave. It's suspicious in the middle of the summer."

"How so?" Dave was thinking of Alice.

"No reason for trouble with the power lines in the summer, unless of course you consider sabotage. You see the direction in which I am heading, don't you, Dave. Winnebagos."

"Shit. I can't open without power. Department of Health."

Dave started for the dining room and the book of reservations. Phonse followed.

"I called the Newfoundland Light and Power, Dave. They're mystified. Absolutely flummoxed."

Dave dialed the first phone number on the list. He recognized the name, a loyal customer. He got an answering machine. "Hello, Mr. Lunz, this is Dave Purcell calling from the Auk. We've had a power failure out here so I'm afraid we will be closed for the evening. I'm sorry about this." Dave didn't like to disappoint an appreciative gourmet like Lunz but really wasn't the least sorry. He would invite Alice to dine with him. They would be alone.

"I don't think we can just stand by waiting for them to make their move, Dave."

"Phonse, what if they never make that move? What if it's not the Winnebagos?" For no reason Dave found Phonse's looming presence extremely aggravating. He needed his dose. One little rail.

"Perhaps you're right, Dave. Perhaps you are right." Phonse must have sensed his agitation. "You make your calls. I'm off to investigate."

Dave heard the kitchen door close. He dashed to the cellar.

In composing his menu for the evening, Dave took many factors into consideration. He was familiar with Alice's palate, her favorite dishes, but knew to be cautious. Freely satisfying the demands of the tongue might later limit its inquisitiveness. Food that was too rich would induce drowsiness or, worse, bloating and vague feelings of illness. Most important, there should be no sense of shame in having overindulged. Shame — glorious, filthy, yelping wet shame was to be the digestif.

Dave held that certain foods had aphrodisiac effects. Like any accomplished cook, he observed curative or tonic properties in particular herbs and spices. He thus imagined that the correct balance of active elements in a meal would make the diner less inhibited and more easily aroused. He kept this to himself, for to declare such was to confess a faith in black magic, in spells and reptilian infusions, in alchemy, and Dave liked to think he believed in reason, in science.

Dave had watched Alice devour plump and sweet Malpeques, the best of all oysters, with some gusto, and knew the alleged action of the creatures to be true. But to start with a platter of the slippery sea delights would be to betray his eagerness. Linguini with anchovy and wilted onions was a delicious and lust-inducing agent but didn't sound right and would wreak souring havoc on the breath. The powerful hormonal aromatics of kidneys or sweetbreads were sure-fire bets to resonate in the glands and stir the amorous juices, but they were not among Alice's preferred noshes.

Partridge! There were two well-hung young birds in the cooler. Partridge was the perfect dish, savory and rich, yet not heavy, and an extremely potent agent given his ultimate purpose. Partridge, seared and then slowly braised in a tart partridgeberry sauce (for double effect), would be the main course.

There was nothing better to open with than caviar; the fecundity of all those eggs, the sheer lavishness of it and the tantalizingly briny scent of beach and gash. Dave had a precious four-ouncer of Iranian Ossetra stashed away for a special occasion. He decided to forgo the appropriate accompaniment of icy vodka in favor of champagne. It wouldn't do to get pissed at the outset.

He knew that chocolate fulfilled or substituted for some base human needs and so dismissed it as an ingredient from his list of dessert possibilities. Dessert was all-important, the final act of sweet spoon and finger-licking before, hopefully, rolling around on the floor like a couple of savages. Tropical fruit was the answer, a nice cleansing contrast to the game, evoking sun, warm water and nakedness. A simple selection of ripe pineapple and mango chunks, sprayed with lime juice and ever so faintly dusted with cayenne (an old trick) with a suggestively runny, creamy salty Camembert on the side. He would have the best Armagnac on hand to work against her inhibitions but would limit himself to one shallow snifter, lest the booze thin the blood he was answering.

Only when heading to the cellar to retrieve the evening's wine (1985 La Tâche in memory of the night he and Alice met) and the champagne did Dave really notice the absence of electricity. He had to find his way in the dark basement with the aid of a flashlight. The kitchen's stoves were propane but all the lighting would be affected. It was perfect, the big dining room all to themselves, lit with dozens of candles. Tonight, he mused, this night. Tonight. Claire, he thought, shaking his head in an effort to banish the image of his wife, an image that, although hazy, as if projected on gauze, was virulently gaining substance.

Even though he was trying to busy his mind with the preparation of his secret potions, he was growing nervous, self-conscious. When he had called Alice with the news that he would close for the night and to invite her to dinner he found himself struggling with his words. Hearing Alice's voice over the phone while imagining her naked body reduced him to a horny teenager. He couldn't remember how one ended a phone call, saying, "All right then, at eight, so it's no problem, well we're on, see ya, bye, all right, eight, good-bye."

But any hope of untying his knotty tongue, of gaining some composure, of playing the suave sophisticate, was lost when Alice entered the kitchen at seven-thirty, a half an hour early.

His head was turned from the spiny works of a pineapple by a gust of burnt summer air across the back of his neck. With a dark chocolate cocktail dress for a sail, Alice let the day's heat carry her into the room. This creature was spinning tendrils around every sinew in his body, tugging at the ropes that held him together. She ran her thumbs under the dress's spaghetti straps, lifted the garment and shifted her body within, allowing Dave a fleeting glance of her breast.

"Sorry I'm early but I had to get out of the house. Phonse and Deb were having a field day making cracks about the outfit." The dress fell back into place. A puff of Alice's scent drifted under Dave's nose.

"Sure," he said.

"I like to get dressed up. I never have the chance. Christ, I could barely get into this thing."

"Sure."

"Do you like it? A bit tarty, hey? Montreal. It's a nipple town, everybody going around with their nipples showing."

Was she trying to cripple Dave, to take him out at the knees? He was a shy man, he thought, this frank talk weakened him. He had to get out of her presence, calm himself.

"Well. I'm hardly, I mean you're so dressed up . . . I . . . well, I was cooking and . . ."

"Do you want to change? You don't have to because of this," Alice said, slowly sweeping her hands over her outfit from her breasts downward to her hips. "Is there anything I can do?"

"Yep. Candles, I guess. Power's still out."

"What is that all about? You'd think they would have the lines fixed by now. Phonse is beside himself, thinks they're coming to get him."

"Thinks who's coming to get him?"

"Who knows? Possibly the tax man. Phonse has always been paranoid, always thinks there are people in the bushes watching him. I don't know how Deb puts up with it."

"Yeah." Dave scurried off to change.

She was so cool, so at ease, and he was so flustered, so inept. What could Alice see in him? How many brilliant Romeos had wooed her in sexy, sensual Montreal? How many tall, thin, dark-haired Latin types, in their leather jackets, Gitanes dangling from their lips, had known exactly what to say, and said it in French! Maybe this was just a pity fuck for Alice, so pathetic did she find her chubby boss.

Looking at himself in the mirror, he saw that his T-shirt was stained with two streaked hand prints. His belt was flapping undone. Who was he kidding? Alice could not possibly find him desirable. And what horror would come over her when he undressed? His hanging gut created a little crease across his waist. Jesus! He was getting tits. Tits! Thank God for candlelight.

Dave dug through what little clothes he owned that still fit. He was never a natty dresser. He didn't know how to buy clothes. The few items he possessed appropriate for such an occasion had been purchased for him by Claire. Claire, who had to dress him up to take him out. He found a pair of light green Italian trousers, a crisp white Lifton shirt, an expensive tie he had never worn (a gift from Claire, their last Christmas, a decidedly chilly celebration it had been). The tie had birds on it. Jays? Finches? No. They were mockingbirds. He pulled on a black blazer and marched back upstairs, a flock of butterflies giving him lift.

Alice had left the kitchen for the dining room, taking the caviar with her. She probably felt she should seize control of the evening if anything was to come of it. Dave drew a deep breath and walked through the swinging doors.

The room was moving, flickering in the light of a hundred candles. Alice had placed them everywhere. She had made a shrine of the zinc bar, its surface reflecting amber into the air. Where she could not find space for the candles on tables she had pulled out chairs. She had employed every tea saucer and side plate to hold the glowing sticks. She laughed.

"When I heard the power was out I ran into Push Through, to Dick's, and bought every candle in the store. I don't guess I've made many friends. They're not big on Phonse or his relatives in there."

Next to the caviar was a frosty bottle of vodka. She had pulled it from the freezer in the kitchen. By the light of the hundred slender flames she looked a specter. Dave felt his blood stir.

"It's beautiful, Alice. It's . . ." Dave couldn't think what to say.

"Is it romantic?"

"Positively," said Dave. He sat down opposite Alice.

"Iranian caviar, Dave?" Alice raised an eyebrow.

"Don't you like caviar?"

"When I think of the caviar wasted on people that don't appreciate it. Briny old fish eggs. You've even got the wooden spoons. How perfect. You are always trying to get things perfect, aren't you, Dave?" She took one of the spoons and harvested a healthy sample of the shiny black stuff from its crystal nest. She extended the spoon to Dave. He opened his mouth. Alice placed the spoon lightly on his tongue. He closed his mouth around it. Slowly, cautiously, Alice withdrew the spoon.

"I hope I don't get winged out on the vodka," she said.

"It was supposed to be champagne."

"Oh, no. Shag champagne. I'm never impressed by champagne. Are you?"

"No, actually, I'm not fond of champagne." It was true.

Alice helped herself to the caviar using the same spoon with which she had just fed Dave. She looked to be crushing the little eggs against the roof of her mouth with her tongue.

"Vodka, Dave?"

Dave poured them each a short tumbler, so cold it had a gelatinous sheen. They clinked glasses and tossed them back, both of them careful not to lose the other's gaze.

"Vodka's probably a good idea, hey? Get a little loose," said Alice.

Dave laughed. It was inexplicably funny. He felt happy. Happy and horny.

"Laugh, will you?" said Alice. "I can't believe it. I'm a nervous wreck here. You're not nervous?"

"Alice, I'm a bag of nerves. I don't know. It's been a long time since I've been on a date." Dave regretted saying this. It was, in a way, bringing up the subject of his wife. Alice seemed not to notice.

"I had a crush on you that first night at Debbie's," she confessed.

"No, you didn't."

"I did. Don't let your head swell. It was probably because you were the first person I'd met in three months who wasn't stuck in the gravity of planet Newfoundland. People can go crazy here, Dave."

Dave was so happy, so relieved. He was in love. He laughed again. He simply couldn't contain his glee.

"Crush is not the word for it, Alice, the way I felt about you. I was . . . I've been dying."

"Eat your caviar."

She offered up another spoonful of little black pearls. Dave pulled the tiny eggs off the spoon and crushed them against the roof of his mouth as Alice had done. They were *perfect*. He looked at Alice's tight and muscular shoulders. She was a strong, substantial person. There was nothing waifish or vulnerable about her at all. He was so tired of weakness, of doubt, of victims, of his own tendency to vacillate, to question. With Alice everything now seemed so certain.

"Dave, will we ever make it to dessert?"

Alice rose from her chair and stood above Dave for a moment, looking down at him before hiking up her dress and straddling his lap. She wound her arms around his neck. Her lips were about to touch his and she paused to smile.

How good it was to kiss her, her tongue pushed against his. He pressed his hand against her back, ran his fingers up to her shoulder and her neck, her fine, slender neck.

Alice suddenly pulled back, sitting upright and letting out a deep sigh.

"Oh, Dave, shit, this is wrong. I don't mean us doing this. We should have done it ages ago. That's the problem.

Well, I just saw us running out of time. I'm such a chicken-shit. I should have jumped your bones ages ago."

Yes, thought Dave. Jump them now. What's stopping you, what's wrong? Jump my bones until they rattle.

"See . . . shit, I feel like . . . anyway, what it is . . . is your wife called yesterday. She's coming up tomorrow. It was supposed to be a surprise."

"Oh," said Dave. He should have been consumed by guilt, should have had doubts about the spot he now found himself in, but he did not. He could feel moist heat coming from between Alice's legs. His cock, now giving the orders, was struggling against his pants.

"I'm sorry. It puts you in a difficult position, I guess," Alice said.

"It does. But, Alice, I want you now. My only thought now is that I should only make matters worse. Let us work toward an emotional calamity. I'm ready for it!"

Alice kissed him on the forehead, her fingers touching his lips, gently opening his mouth.

There was a knock at the front door. They froze.

"Did you reach all the reservations?" whispered Alice.

"I got a couple of answering machines."

"Did you put a sign on the door?"

Dave shook his head. The rapping came again, more insistent.

"They'll figure it out soon enough and then they'll go away," Dave said. They sat in silence for a moment. Dave drank in Alice's scent, her perfume mingling with the flush of her skin. He kissed her neck.

The beating returned, now from the window, which

warbled under the pounding. Alice stood and walked to the front door.

The sexual anticipation was exhilarating. The waiting, the curiosity, he could taste it. Dave's body was talking to him in urgent whispers: "Kiss her, touch her, squeeze her." He was transported, his senses heightened, there was power in his limbs. He felt younger. The world had, in a few moments, ceased being such a puzzle.

Alice returned accompanied by a bowl of a man — a short, round balding myopic. Binoculars hung from a reddened roll of flesh that marked the junction of his head and torso. The heavy optical instrument rested on his ample belly. The sides of his head were thinly covered with wisps of orange hair. His flesh was reminiscent of a badly plucked chicken. He didn't speak, he squeaked.

"Car's gone. Towing?"

Dave had no idea what the man meant.

"His car has vanished, Dave," said Alice. "He thinks it's been stolen."

"They'll have to consult dental records if the crowd from the Upper Road have it." Dave didn't care about the man's car. He wanted this round fellow quickly out of the way.

"How dreadful," he squeaked again. "You don't expect it here."

It was the hollow myth of Newfoundland again. The people were all supposed to be so sweet and colorful but never dangerous, the good poor. This was Canada's Happy Province. I'll introduce you to some of the car cannibals, thought Dave. They'd club you like a seal pup and sell your organs for the price of a dozen beer.

"Could I please use your phone?"

Dave nodded a reluctant yes. Alice had taken her seat, her romantic impulse rapidly diminishing. The mood was in jeopardy. Dave looked at the round man. He seemed very carefree, very pleased with himself for a man whose car had just been stolen.

"You're taking the news well," Dave observed bitterly.

The man dialed a couple of numbers, stopped, listened, held the phone away from his ear and tried again. "To be honest," he said, "the car hardly seems to matter. I've seen Tasker's sulphureous. What a day!" He continued to struggle with the phone.

Had the Push Cove monster again risen from beneath the waves?

"You saw the duck?" asked Dave, needing more detail.

"Saw it! If it hadn't got dark I would have had a close-up of the head. It was just sitting there on the water, so peaceful. Hey, this phone isn't working."

The decoy was adrift in Push Cove, incriminating evidence waiting to be retrieved. Rumors of the rare bird were one thing. Proof of carefully planned and executed deceit was another.

Alice went to the man's assistance.

"It's true, Dave. The phones are dead."

Dave didn't care about the phone. He had to find the decoy and destroy it. If the decoy was discovered it would be over with Alice. She had expressed bewilderment at her sister's relationship with Phonse. Alice didn't like mischief makers. And Alice was all that mattered now.

"So the duck was close to shore, then?" Dave asked, seeking specifics.

"Oh, no," said the little man, "fifty yards out at least. What am I going to do? How will I get back to St. John's?"

Alice was looking decidedly unsexy. She was rubbing her exposed shoulders as if they were cold. She was picking at her dress, suddenly uncomfortable in the garment. It was the duck's fault.

"I'll tell you what," said Dave. "I'll go to the neighbors and phone a taxi."

"That will cost a fortune, a taxi all the way from here into St. John's!" the man said.

"What, then?" Dave barked. Alice and the man recoiled.

"I was going to call my wife, the police."

"Don't bother with the police." Dave was improvising. "They won't be very happy if you call them out here now."

"But shouldn't they know right away, put out an all-points-bulletin or something?" the man asked, puzzled by Dave's insight into the likes and dislikes of the Royal Newfoundland Constabulary.

"Listen," said Dave, "my brother is a cop, very big with the police brotherhood. Let's just say things will go a lot smoother if you leave this to me, hey?" This was an enormous lie. Lloyd was indeed familiar with the police, but in ways Dave did not think it wise to reveal. Both Alice, surprised by the news, and the unwelcome visitor believed it. "Write down your wife's phone number."

The man picked up a pen and scribbled, handing Dave the slip of paper.

Dave looked at Alice. He wanted to say, "Never mind your disappointment, it is half the measure of my own." He wanted to say, "For the first time in years and years I am going to take care of everything." But he simply said, "I won't be long."

Dave charged through the swinging doors.

He had known from the moment the round man had said the duck was fifty yards from shore that he would need the shotgun from the cellar. He would go to Phonse's and call the round man's wife, but only after blowing the wooden duck out of the water. Alice wanted him. The curse of the duck, of the lie that had propped up the charade of the Auk, needed to be purged. He could have no secrets from Alice. It could not be coincidence that Phonse's decoy had shown up at the very moment he was going to settle things with her. The duck was trouble, an evil juju, looming forever over Dave. It was his contract with the devil. They had been playing games with God, resurrecting the dead, and if Dave did not soon repent God would continue this torment. Blasting the duck to smithereens would forever end the Faustian bargain.

Dave forgot to bring the flashlight and so had to feel his way, blind, into the cellar. He ran his hands along the stone wall, moist with condensation, and found the gun. Its barrel was cool in his hands, the metal telling. Crouching, he felt for and retrieved a lead-heavy box of shells. And, for the first time in his life, Dave felt compelled to fire the weapon, wanted the flash and the crash of the powder blast, wanted to feel his ears ring.

16

Without electricity to feed the exterior lights of the Auk, Dave stepped outdoors into utter blackness. He paused for a moment, letting his eyes adjust. He thought of the Svetkov lamps. They could be put to good use here. Fumbling, he pulled four shells out of the box and let it drop to the ground. He stuck three shells in his pants pocket and, breeching the gun, another in its barrel chamber. The shell fit the barrel so perfectly, so cozily. The weight of the gun gave Dave balance. He was more sure-footed, closer, tighter to the earth. His grip was firm on the stock. Dave remembered a line from a poem, "snug as a gun," was it? And this was a fine gun. A gift from his friend and cadre, Alphonse Murphy.

Dave wanted to run but restricted himself to a close trot, rapid little baby steps. There was really no call for it, but he made every effort to be silent, holding his breath, testing the ground gently with his feet. He felt he was stalking something.

The recent heat seemed to have drawn resins and gums

out of the tress, the air was heady with high vapors — retsina, frankum and menthol menace.

In the gloom he was briefly lost. The woods out here were radically transformed at night. Dave would never have accepted this only a year earlier, but now he knew that sinister forces rearranged the world under cover of darkness. They shuffled the trees and rocks, put up obstructions in an effort to lure you deeper into the forest. Squinting, Dave made out vague patterns in the gloom. There was a black hole in a black wall — the trail to the sea.

Dave was stupid not to have thought about the errant decoy when Phonse mentioned having lost it. He should have known that it was adrift on Push Cove. This was the right thing to do, take action, deal with the situation before it dealt with him. And it would be fine to shoot something.

Dave could finally hear the lapping of waves. He was making progress. Would he be able to spot the duck, though? He needed only a shadow, a silhouette against the sea's luminescence. He remembered what his father told him about shotguns: never aim, simply point. Just a glimpse was all he needed. The duck was no doubt moving toward the beach, washing ashore. If it was close enough the wide pulse of searing shot, of spicy lead pepper, would inflict enough damage to capsize it, to disfigure it, turning it from a duck into driftwood, filling it with wormy holes. He would use all the shells, firing into the sea, bringing the matter to its end.

Spruce branches were at his face, scratching him, making him itch. Dave had wandered from the main trail, down a rabbit run. This was not good. He wanted to shoot the gun now, get it over with and return, triumphant, to Alice.

He spun around to make his way back to the trail when he heard something moving in the woods. He froze in his tracks. Close behind him there was hard, heavy, quick breathing. Someone else was coming down the trail. Had Alice followed him? Was the round man returning for a last look at the duck? Dave stood perfectly still.

The figure was neither the Round One nor Alice. It was a wiry man who seemed lost, unable to decide whether to go up or down the trail. The man sighed in exasperation. Perhaps he was looking for something, a birder who had lost his precious little list.

It suddenly struck Dave as wrong, as unjust, that he, the armed owner of this property, should be cowering in the bushes from some bird-watching twit. The course of action was clear, so clear and so funny that Dave almost laughed out loud. The birders were beginning to piss him off anyway, he was too reliant on them and tired of sucking up. It was time to reclaim some dignity.

With three short silent steps he was almost on top of the man. It was an intoxicating thrill, standing there, hovering, unseen. He was a ghost. His shotgun raised, Dave stepped into the path.

"What the fuck are you doing, Jack?" Dave's voice was not his own. It was deeper, raspy, sandpaper.

The figure convulsed with fright, his arms shot out, a choking sound came from his throat. Dave felt ashamed of himself. It was a terrible thing to do to someone. Dave squinted to make out the face, meaning to apologize, when he saw, clasped in the man's hand, the distinct outline of a pistol.

"Drop it," said Dave. The demand had not come from his rational mind. It was an absurd reflex, something retrieved from all the bad movies he had seen.

The pistol hit the ground.

"Please." It was the voice of a young man, thin, tremulous with desperate fear.

Dave couldn't think what to do.

"Winnebago?" he asked. It seemed the only possibility.

"I don't know" — the voice was verging on sobs — "I don't know . . . is it Harrier? Is it code 12 yellow? I don't know the response. Please." The man was now crying softly, unable to answer a bizarre riddle on which he thought his life depended. Dave wanted to reassure the man but was now growing fearful himself. What if the man went for his pistol? Dave couldn't possibly fire on him.

Dave tried again. "Are you with Winnebago?"

"No. I'm with the orange unit."

The orange unit. Who on earth were they?

Dave couldn't take the man back to the Auk but thought he must do something, and so he turned the intruder around and put the shotgun to his back. Dave marched him on to Phonse's.

Candlelight was visible from Phonse's house. Dave told the young man to knock on the front door. Deb came to the door carrying a candle.

"Dave! What in God's name are you doing?"

"Get Phonse!"

Phonse had evidently been lurking just around the corner. He came to the door quickly, pushing Deb back into the house. "Get inside," Phonse told her.

Deb was reluctant to comply. She hissed something at Phonse. He took her aside for a moment and she disappeared. Phonse stepped from the house, closing the door behind him.

"Brilliant, Dave, a hostage!"

A hostage? Dave didn't want to take a hostage. He wanted to go back to the Auk and pretend nothing had happened. Phonse was scurrying toward the shed.

"Come on."

Whimpering slightly, the hostage did as he was told. Dave followed, feeling something of a hostage himself.

By the time Dave and the stranger were inside the shed Phonse had already equipped himself with an electric lantern and a rifle. He indicated that the man should sit on an old sawhorse. Phonse shone the light in the man's face, and the young fellow squinted painfully. The hostage looked as young as he sounded, his skin still pinkish, in his twenties, Dave guessed. He was almost handsome, but his eyes were too close together, his nose too thin. He wasn't from Newfoundland. He looked Canadian. It was all too scary; Dave wanted out.

"I found him in the bushes by the Auk, Phonse. He had a pistol. Let's just call the cops."

"No telephone, Dave." Phonse wasn't paying much attention to Dave. He was busy sizing up his trophy, examining the man's head as if he planned on cutting into it. "You surprise me, Dave. Honestly, I didn't think you had it in you."

Dave tried to resist the sensation, but he felt a touch of pride. He had finally impressed Alphonse Murphy, who was now glowering at the sorry figure who trembled on the sawhorse.

"Winnebago?" Phonse barked.

The man started to bawl, shaking with his sobs.

"He doesn't seem to know what that means, Phonse. He says he's with the orange unit."

"The orange unit?" Phonse scratched his chin.

"He's probably just . . ."

"How many of you?" He was stern.

"Sixteen," said the hostage.

What was going on? Sixteen of who? Were there fifteen more men in the woods with guns?

"Listen, laddie-o." There was crisp, certain menace in Phonse's voice, a tone Dave had never before heard from his friend. Phonse was a tough character, Dave realized. God only knew what he was capable of. "You telling me there are fifteen of you fucks out there?" Phonse jabbed his rifle into the man's ribs.

The man nodded. It didn't seem as though he could speak.

Phonse's head was bobbing up and down, as if he had finally figured it out. He paced, humphing to himself. Dave waited for the answer. Phonse went to the shed door, opened it and quickly fired three rounds in the air. Dave jumped. The report was deafening inside the shed. Phonse ran back to the man on the sawhorse.

"Well, now they know we mean business. Who the fuck are you with?"

"I'm with CSIS," the man whimpered.

CSIS! The Canadian Security and Intelligence Service. Canada's spies and spy catchers, baby spooks, boy scouts of the international sleuthing trade. Phonse looked at Dave.

"What in the name of Christ do *they* want, Dave?"

It must have been Phonse's firing of the rifle. The air in the shed, already scented with burnt gunpowder, was filling with that Burgundy background, the smell of shit. As Phonse had said, there were two kinds of people in the world. Dave thought that to qualify for CSIS one would have to be in the Churchillian class of locked sphincters, but the young prisoner had clearly soiled himself in fear.

"I suppose they want the R.S.V., Phonse." Dave turned to the young man. "Do you want the R.S.V.?"

The young man tried to speak. Only gurgling noises came out. Phonse stuck the rifle to the poor fellow's temple, grinding the tip of the barrel against the skin.

"Answer the question. Are you fuckers after the R.S.V.?"

"Phonse! For Christ's sake." Seeing the young man suffer was sickening Dave. A nausea he had never known was turning his stomach juices sour. Evil was in the air. Perhaps the story the locals told about the Irish family was true. Perhaps there was a force beneath the soil here that worked on the darker reaches of the mind, driving men to unspeakable acts of violence. Phonse would pull the trigger, the top of the hostage's head would crack open like a soft-boiled egg. They would feast on the poor soul's brains (professional curiosity for gastronome Dave) before disappearing into the woods. Dave shook his head, trying to clear it of black nonsense.

The gun did its job. The young man managed a few words. "I . . . I don't know the response . . . to R.S.V."

"The *submarine!*" Phonse screamed, his lips almost touching the man's ear.

The man's head dropped. He was trying to suppress convulsions of terror, shaking almost as though he was laughing. "They . . . they . . . want . . . the lights. Please don't kill me."

"Look." Dave laid a hand on the man's shoulder. The man flinched. "No one is going to kill anybody."

Phonse glowered at Dave and then gave a flick of his head. Dave followed him to the doors of the shed. Phonse whispered.

"Dave, I am not planning on shooting this poor lad, but don't you think it would help matters if he at least imagines it's in the cards?"

Dave was astonished. "No, Phonse, I don't." Dave's voice was raised. Phonse shushed him. "I don't want any part in terrorizing this fellow. It's making me ill. We're already in enough trouble."

"What trouble are we in, Dave?" Phonse asked the question with a rare ferocity, as though he had finally lost all patience with his ridiculous neighbor.

"Kidnapping, forcible confinement . . . and clearly there's something funny about the lights."

Phonse looked skyward in exasperation. "Dave, one: this fellow was on your property in the middle of the night with a gun in his hands. Two: why should we believe anything he says? Three: if he is really with CSIS, he should be prepared for this kind of thing. This kind of treatment is probably in the man's contract."

Dave thought about his. He wondered if in fact, in some convoluted bureaucratese, being taken hostage and tortured was a part of the man's job description. Surely, given the nature of his work, he must have signed a dozen waivers. Having worked for the federal government, Dave knew it wasn't such a far-fetched notion.

"Four: I can always say I tried to call the police but the phones were down. I was just holding him until I could get help."

It all made sense. Phonse was right again. He was thinking clearly while Dave's head was filling with visions of gunplay and cannibalism.

"I still can't help you, Phonse. I can't do this."

"Dave, perhaps I should remind you that you were the one that captured him."

Captured? This really was a nightmare. What kind of a mess had Dave got himself into? This was far more serious than anything that had come before, it was worse than the duck hoax, worse than the trip in the R.S.V. Their hostage had been armed. So, then, were his fifteen friends outside. What was to stop them from shooting their way in, pumping the shed full of lead? The authorities could reason their way out of the violence the same way Phonse had justified keeping the man at gunpoint. They were CSIS, after all; they didn't make it their business to explain anything to anybody. Phonse and Dave would simply be *disappeared*. Lloyd said such things happened, that the police routinely planted incriminating evidence, bullied witnesses, took bribes, but Dave hadn't believed him until now.

"Phonse, I'm scared."

Not a hint of sympathy registered on Phonse's face.

Phonse walked back to his shit-stinking hostage. The lantern in his hand was throwing spooky shadows against the big bare walls of the shed. The hostage became a hunched troll looming over the room. Bits of chain hanging from metal bars, winches, tanks of acetylene were found by the swinging beam of light and projected into monstrous hazards, wildly swinging booms, a gallows, spider webs, tentacles, prison bars.

Dave had been so impressed by Phonse's shed, had so admired his neighbor's ingenuity, his command of lathes and drills, of calipers and meters. They were now the workings of a torture chamber. The drums and barrels were full of noxious fluids, highly-volatile liquids waiting to ignite. They were no doubt this moment leaking poisonous vapors, mind-muddling gases.

There was nothing to keep Dave from leaving. He could bolt. He could walk out the door and run back to the restaurant and Alice. Alice, what was she thinking now? That Dave had been overcome by guilt and taken the Round Man's appearance as opportunity to flee? And the decoy. It was still bobbing around Push Cove. He could hardly head back down to the beach with a loaded shotgun in his hands with the woods full of armed agents. Even if he chose to head back to the restaurant, how would they know he wasn't dangerous, carrying a concealed weapon? Would he put his hands over his head like a surrendering soldier? That would be admitting that he had done something wrong.

"Phonse?"

He was tying the man to the sawhorse. Lashing him down with a length of rough, hairy rope. Phonse had laid down his rifle but the man was so terrorized he made no attempt to escape. The deranged geezer was evidently planning on keeping his hostage for some time. What did he have in mind? A deal with CSIS? "Freedom for your man in return for immunity." The story about Uri Svetkov might well have been a lie; perhaps Phonse had stolen the plans for the submarine and the precious, unearthly lights from the good guys.

"Phonse?" Dave was hovering near him now, seeking guidance and protection.

Phonse finished tying the man down. Strangely, the bonds seemed to settle the hostage. It was as if being tied down gave him an excuse for his powerlessness, completed the formal theater of having been captured. Dave thought that he too might feel better if Phonse took him prisoner. No, it was a ridiculous idea.

Phonse grabbed Dave by the arm, pulling him toward the fuel barrels and the bale of cocaine. "Dave. Take some cocaine."

"Are you mad, Phonse? Clear heads prevail."

"Dave, I hate to say this, but drugs agree with you."

This was a terrible thought. Did Dave need artificial courage, chemical inspiration? Yes.

The first line's immediate effects were all wrong. Phonse dashed off into the shadows. Dave could hear him bolting windows shut, fortifying the shed, digging through boxes and crates in search of ammunition. Dave was frozen. Matters suddenly seemed much worse. A painful and ignominious death became a certainty. All was lost. He needed to talk with his father, settle things with him before he died. Alice would never be his. He even wanted to patch things up with Larry. Anxiety permeated his very being, the space between every cell in his sorry body was filling up with a foul black acid. He was becoming corruption and death, a vessel for absolute misery. The situation was impossible, the calculation necessary to find a way out of the maze was beyond him, he couldn't get his thoughts straight.

He inhaled another line.

This was the moment when the men were separated from the boys, the critical moment when the caper succeeded or failed, it was make or break. Would Dave be remembered as one of thousands of phantoms in the federal bureaucracy, a failed restaurateur, or a bandit, an outlaw? To go down in flames, in a blaze of glory, was the ultimate revenge against his former colleagues at Fisheries. They would see the picture of his bullet-riddled corpse in the papers and say, "We never guessed for a second that he was involved in that sort of thing." "He seemed like such a quiet man. To discover that he was a major player in international espionage. It's extraordinary." Dying at the hands of the Canadian government was the only way Dave could square things up with Newfoundland. It would be a grand gesture of resistance, a former collaborator going over to the other side, betraying the colonial master. Let Claire have her political talk shows, her numbing verbiage — Dave would be at the center of things, where the action was. He inhaled another line.

"What's the plan, Phonse?"

Phonse smiled. "I must try that cocaine sometime, Dave."

"I don't think it's for you, Phonse. You're just not sad enough. And another thing, we had better get rid of it before the doors come off their hinges and cops charge in. I don't imagine it will help our case."

"It had never occurred to me, Dave. Good thinking. Shovel it into the stove."

Dave dragged the bale to the fat stove at the rear of the shed. All his abuse hadn't even dented the cache. He opened the heavy door, filled the stove with kindling. The dry, brittle pieces soon created a bed of embers, rippling with orange and yellow heat. He threw a split birch junk in and it immediately caught.

But CSIS was not interested in the cocaine. Perhaps, thought Dave, he could preserve an amount sufficient to get him through the next few trying months — a half-gram a day for ninety days, that would be what? Forty-five grams. Make it fifty. No, he should wean himself. Forty grams, then. He could stash it all over the shed in undetectable two-gram portions, at twenty points of the compass so he would remember where to find it. Sixteen points would be easier on the circle, south-southwest followed by south. Twenty went into sixteen how many times? Stumped by the mathematics of addiction, Dave knew he should torch the lot.

There was nothing with which to scoop up the white powder and so Dave used his hands. The cocaine burned easily, the crystals flashing slightly as they passed through the flame. Trails of smoke found Dave's nostrils. The burning cocaine had a nasty metallic smell, a perfume of panic.

Dave emptied the bale but for one last handful of powder. He was fighting his powerful need to preserve this last measure of the drug when Phonse knelt beside him. He turned to face his friend and got a terrific start. Phonse had covered his face and hair with black motor grease. Only the whites of his eyes shone through the glossy petroleum mask.

"I hate to leave you, Dave, but you've got to stay here for a while. Stall them."

"How?"

"My first suggestion is that you fire the occasional round into the bushes. Send a few over their heads. Keep them pinned down."

Dave shook his head. The desire to fire a gun had left him.

"I didn't think so." Phonse hung his head. He seemed unhappy with the alternative course of action. "I suppose you will have to talk to them. Demand proof that they are who they say they are and so on. Negotiate. That will give me a few minutes."

"What are you going to do, Phonse?"

For the first time since Dave had known him, Phonse was lost for words. He shrugged, looking defeated.

"Phonse," Dave said, "you must have a Plan B. Always have a Plan B."

Phonse smiled. "Dave, old man, that's surely the truth." He stepped quickly to the tunnel and was gone.

Dave knew Phonse could never hand over the R.S.V., certainly not to the government. What he would do to avoid such was beyond Dave's imagining. He picked himself off the ground, his knees creaking, and walked to the hostage.

"I'm sorry about all this," Dave said.

The young man looked up at him with profound scorn. "The fuck you are. I won't cooperate."

Dave was relieved that Phonse had bound the man. It was pathetic that the prisoner should now, with Phonse out of the picture, finally display courage. The young CSIS agent likely knew deadly hand-to-hand combat techniques and would happily beat the piss out of the sorry figure that had caused him such humiliation. The hostage would also have to construct a very different tale of his capture to save face. He would never admit to compliance and weakness but would report brutality at Dave's hand. Everyone did this, Dave realized, changed their story to account for decisions that were cowardly or misguided.

Dave was chuckling about it when thin beams of intense white light made a pincushion of the shed, enveloping him in a cat's cradle of sizzling rays. A crackling amplified voice came from a megaphone.

"Mr. Purcell."

Dave looked at the hostage, who was now grinning defiantly at him.

"Mr. Purcell, Mr. Murphy we know you are in there. I am a law enforcement agent. I have reason to believe you are holding one of my men against his will."

They still thought Phonse was in the shed. He must have made a clean escape. Hunched to avoid the anticipated hail of bullets, Dave shuffled to the large doors.

Through a small gap he peered out. Toward the top of the lane he could make out two cars and a big four-wheel-drive. The four-wheel-drive had a bank of spotlights mounted on its roof, all pointing at the shed. Dave could just make out figures moving about the cars. In the woods directly across from the shed, the edges of the spotlights' beam caught something reflective. A sniper's watch, Dave guessed. They aren't that good, he thought.

Law enforcement. He was going to be arrested. Suddenly Phonse's logic was as full of holes as the shed. The old codger was no sage, he had been improvising, getting himself out of a spot by sacrificing his erstwhile friend. Dave couldn't say they didn't know who the hostage was and didn't believe his claim to be with CSIS. They could make up whatever story they liked to implicate Dave and Phonse in some trumped-up arms and narcotics importing scam. Dave was going to jail. He remembered the remaining cocaine and dashed to the stove. As Dave passed him the hostage grumbled. Dave heard only "settle with you . . ." It wasn't Dave acting but Phonse acting through him. He rapped the man hard on the back of the head with his knuckles.

"You're going to settle nothing with nobody because I'm going to shoot you in a moment," Dave said and laughed.

The hostage gasped, thinking perhaps that he had made a fatal assessment of his remaining captor.

Dave scooped up the last of the cocaine from the bale and, sticking both nostrils in the pile, snorted what he could before throwing the remains in the fading fire. Hearing the savage snorting, the hostage started whimpering again. Was Dave using the evil drug to steel himself for the final act, a murder?

Dave gathered up the empty bale and forced it through the stove door. It smoldered, looking for a moment like it was going to smother the fire, and then ignited all at once in a quiet explosion of scarlet. A great wave of relief came over Dave. A curse was lifted. He never wanted to see the horrible powder again.

"Mr. Purcell, I don't think I need tell you . . ." It was the voice from outside. Dave dashed to the shed doors. The massive dosage of cocaine was a mistake. He felt his heart pounding at his chest. He shouted through the gap in the doors.

"Listen, get that guy out of the woods. How do I know who the fuck you are!"

There was no response for a moment, then the amplified voice again. "He is coming out now."

A figure emerged from the woods with his hands over his head. He was wearing a jumpsuit and a headset with a microphone. A busy utility belt hung about his hips. It's his Bat Belt, Dave thought, he's probably got a Bat Rope in there. This was Fuck-Up Man's last stand. The man from the woods looked prepared for either mountain climbing or space travel. He walked slowly up the lane toward the parked vehicles but sprinted the last three yards before diving, dramatically, out of sight.

Despite the gravity of the situation, Dave could not suppress a belly laugh. He turned to his hostage.

"You guys don't get a lot of opportunities like this, I guess?"

It wasn't so funny. There were men in the bushes sighting rifles who didn't often have the opportunity to fire at real flesh and blood, men who longingly spent hours on the shooting range popping holes in paper villains. Picking off fat Dave would be easy.

"Mr. Purcell. I don't want you and Mr. Murphy to be alarmed. We know this has been a misunderstanding. We know of Mr. Svetkov's involvement and don't blame you for anything."

The voice was trying to comfort Dave, to reassure him, but the words, distorted, surrounded by electronic noise, bouncing through the trees lost their meaning in transit. No one had ever needed a megaphone to tell the truth. Dave heard careful footsteps on the roof.

He was supposed to stall. He shouted through the gap.

"Are you nuts? Christ, I find some guy with a gun wandering around in the woods behind my restaurant and you tell me not be alarmed." Dave was pleased with himself. He was arguing the case Phonse had presented. Where was Phonse now? "How can I trust you?" he shouted. It was too funny and he laughed again. The cocaine was flooding his veins with cockiness. Dave's mirth was distressing to the hostage. The threat of a shooting, the smack in the back of the head and now this deviant glee. Dave again appeared to be a drug-crazed killer. The hostage kept up his quiet sobbing.

"David?" A new voice, familiar, was coming over the megaphone. "I'm so sorry about this. Please listen to the man. No one will get hurt."

"Claire?" Dave shouted.

"I'm so sorry, David, the thing with Larry was a big mix-up, I want to — She was cut off.

The thing with Larry? Larry had been fucking Claire! Or more correctly, Dave was sure, Claire had been fucking Larry. Fuck-Up Man was a cuckold. Not that he was jealous of Larry or that he really cared any more who Claire fucked, but he was stung that something had been going on behind his back and that he was too naive, too stupid to sense anything. It explained so much, Claire's long absence from St. John's, Larry's weird behavior with the woman from Montreal. She was a cover, a beard of sorts. Claire had said it: "Larry is not as stupid as he seems." They had both been trying to tell him.

"Mr. Purcell. I've given your wife our commitment that no action will be taken and we understand she is on television."

So that was it. He would have been long dead, bombed or gassed or shot in the back, if it wasn't for Claire, an influential imam from the temple of buzz. She had come all this way, come home, only to find herself negotiating the terms of Dave's surrender to the police. No doubt she was telling them how mixed up he was, how he had a drinking problem. The man with the megaphone was still talking.

"We don't want any trouble. I'm coming down now. I want to talk to you and Mr. Murphy."

They wanted to talk to Dave first, trying to get to Phonse through him. They judged, Dave supposed, that he would be the more reasonable of the two. They must have had them under surveillance for some months now. Phonse had spotted footprints in the snow back in the spring. What else did they know? Did they know about Dave and Alice, had they told Claire? Did they know about the duck caper, or about the errant decoy bobbing so dangerously atop the chill waters of Push Cove?

"I'm coming down now."

Dave looked through the gap. It was Cortini. The spotlights gave the scene an eerie cast, burning objects out of space. Cortini, preceded by the long shadow of his form, seemed a paper cutout. He had his arms raised, not over his head but in front of him, as if to say "I am unarmed." The powerful backlighting prohibited Dave from reading any expression on Cortini's face. Cortini stopped in the crabgrass clearing, ten yards from the shed doors.

"Mr. Purcell, I'm coming in now."

Cortini couldn't come in! Dave was to stall them, otherwise they would immediately start the search for Phonse. Seeing Dave was alone, Cortini would probably flatten him with a surgical karate chop to the neck, or drive Dave's nose up into his brains with the palm of his hand. These people were trained in such matters.

"No!" Dave barked. "You stay there. I'll come out and talk to you."

What could possibly have put him in such a spot? How could someone so disinclined to action be at the center of a standoff with the police? This was not Dave Purcell's destiny. He was sure of that. Fate, he saw now, was an impossibly Byzantine matrix of possibilities into which fools were invited to enter. Step from your line and you could become entangled.

The lights were much brighter outside the shed. They startled Dave so that he stumbled slightly as if anticipating a stair that wasn't there. The illumination painted the grass and the spruce trees an inappropriate green. The ground didn't seem quite there, the blades of grass made taller against their shadows. His face to the lights, he could no longer make out the vehicles up the lane or the spectral forms hovering about them. But he could feel many eyes focused intently on his movements, his gestures, all waiting for a sudden motion. Dave supposed this was how actors felt on the stage. He had the leading role. He would have waved to the crowd but worried the move might be mistaken for something hostile.

He was now five feet in front of Cortini but still could not make out his eyes. The faceless figure let his arms down slowly to his side. He was over six feet tall, trim. Dave guessed that this man must love his work.

"Please tell me what is going on here, Mr. Cortini."

"My name isn't Cortini. It's Partington. You remember me from the restaurant?"

"An alias! A nom de guerre! What fun. And yes, I remember you. You were very conspicuous. No drinks."

"I'll try to remember that the next time." There was sarcasm in his voice. He didn't appreciate being told his business.

"Are you really from CSIS?"

"Where did you get that idea?"

"Your man told me."

"We had hoped to keep you out of this, Mr. Purcell." Partington turned his head toward the shed, enabling Dave to discover a contemptuous pale blue in the man's eyes. "We don't blame you for any of it."

"Any of what?"

"Stealing the design for the lights."

"Phonse didn't steal anything. He was partners with Svetkov, they were going to build the R.S.V. together. Svetkov took off."

"What's the R.S.V.?" Partington sounded worried.

"The Recreational Submarine Vehicle, of course."

"What's that?"

"Well . . . it's . . . a tiny little submarine."

Dave could tell that he had taken something very precious from Partington, the privileged and protected knowledge of what was happening, the narrative, the trajectory and meaning of events. Dave was probably the only person in the world who now knew what was going on. "Have you seen the lights, Mr. Partington?"

"No. But I know what they are. I'm certain I'd recognize one if I saw it."

"You would. They are quite unlike any light I have ever seen. They allow you to . . . how should I put this, see into things."

"How did you know they were for submarines?"

"We didn't." (There. He was in league with Alphonse Murphy. And proud of it.) "You see, Phonse — Mr. Murphy — knew you people were watching him, but he thought you were from the Winnebago Corporation, he thought you were trying to steal his plans for the submarine."

Partington stiffened. "It's all been a big mistake then, hasn't it?" Clearly Partington didn't enjoy saying this.

"It often is. I've got a couple of questions for you, Mr. Cortini, or Partington or whatever your name is. What did you tell Dr. Speidel that day that put him in such a foul mood? And secondly, and more importantly, I suppose, what is my wife doing up there?" Dave was stalling; he was doing well.

"The presence of the bird watchers in the area was limiting our actions. We needed them out of the picture. Dr. Speidel wasn't always an ornithologist. He specialized in the study of humans during the war. I'll spare you the details. We told him if he didn't play along, we would be obliged to inform some very interested parties about his sordid past. I don't want it said that we have anything against birds, Mr. Purcell. CSIS supports birds and we always endeavor to be an environmentally friendly agency."

Though it should have been the least of his worries, Dave was relieved they didn't know that the duck was a fake. Even if they did charge him with espionage, with treason, he and Phonse still would have pulled off the Great Duck Caper.

"As for your wife, we found her not more than two hours ago. She was driving along the road, heading for your restaurant. It's entirely coincidental. I don't believe she knows anything about any of this. She was going to surprise you. It's your wedding anniversary. Perhaps you had forgotten." Partington smirked.

Their anniversary. Dave looked at the ground and tried to remember the date. He wasn't even sure of the year.

The shed doors crashed open. Dragging the sawhorse, to which he was still loosely attached, the young hostage bounced on his feet for a moment before falling forward, landing on his face. Dave looked to Partington. Partington looked to his bound man. What perversions, what indignities, had his man suffered at the hands of his captors? The hostage rolled to his side and shouted.

"The other one's got away."

The woods were suddenly alive with white lights. A crossfire of narrow beams blinded Dave. There was a cacophony of radio static, shouted commands and heavy footfalls. Dave was jostled by someone and spun around. A man screamed. Dave shielded his eyes from the light. A man in a jumpsuit went charging out of the bushes toward the Auk, a canister in his belt gushing clouds of smoke or gas. The man was trying desperately to remove it when he collapsed, succumbing to the gas. Fellow agents ran to his assistance but were driven back by the acrid smoke. Dave could taste the stuff, it burnt his throat and made his eyes water. As he turned away a body fell from the sky. It was the man from the roof, landing on his shoulder with a loud crack of bones and crumpling like a puppet.

A giant was standing next to Dave. He flinched, expecting to be suddenly dispatched with the deadly karate chop. It never came. Partington or Cortini — Dave realized that neither of the monikers was genuine — trotted over to his tied man and knelt beside him, demanding more information. Now two men were at Dave's side, firmly gripping his arms. There was a cackling of walkie-talkies. The crabgrass clearing was full of people. There were more than sixteen men, at least thirty. Dave was being turned away from the shed and led toward the light and the cars at the top of the lane. He was preceded by the round birder from the restaurant, who was loudly protesting his treatment and gagging on the smoke. The rough hands on his arms lifted Dave slightly, so that his feet only lightly touched the ground. Inexplicably he felt at ease. These men would now determine his future; he didn't have to make any decisions. He would cooperate, offer no resistance. Dave had done his part and was utterly without remorse.

As he neared the cars at the top of the lane the lights were brighter still, the gas had caused tears to stream from his burning eyes. Dave collided with a figure he could not see. Alice slid her arms around his neck, just managing to kiss him squarely on the mouth before his guards forced him onward. He could hear, but not see, Claire.

"David! Who is that woman? David?"

A big hand on top of his head pushed him down and into the backseat of a car. A senseless two-way radio squawked urgently from the dash. "We've got three men down!"

Then came the explosion.

It was distant but still loud enough to crack the air, to painfully percuss Dave's eardrum. The big hand left Dave's head, enabling him to see the orange flames rising above the trees near the beach. Deb's scream pierced the air.

"Phonse!"

Dave's captors abandoned him; the crowd seemed called to the flames. Dave was among a crush of bodies that first trotted, then ran to the beach.

The beach was lined with people: the CSIS agents, Alice, Deb, the round man, the hostage, all studying the burning fuel atop the waters of Push Cove. The force of the blast had dispersed the fuel, and pools of flame danced and flashed over the shallow black and blue swells.

So Phonse had blown up the R.S.V., choosing death rather than surrender. The ultimate Plan B.

Dave staggered through the crowd. They were hypnotized by the spectacle of the burning water, the apocalyptic vision. He looked for Claire. She was gone. Had she really been there? Had he just imagined her voice?

He surveyed Push Cove, hoping to see a bit of floating rubble, Phonse's punt, any indication that his dear friend had survived the blast. All he saw was the flaming outline of a duck, drifting through a pool of the burning fuel as if paddling peacefully across a pond. The decoy's head dropped as if it was falling asleep. It rolled over and was gone.

Dave found Deb apart from the cluster of bodies. She was scanning the beach for her husband, clutching herself, her arms wound tightly about her torso as if fending off a chill, her face painted amber by the lambent sea.

"Plan B," Dave said out loud.

17

Dave enjoyed his rented truck as a boy would. He liked being up above the traffic, bouncing big with the bumps, his arms spread wide to hold the broad steering wheel. The thought of a long-distance drive crossed his mind: take the one-ton truck up to Montreal and Alice, or perhaps all the way down to Washington to give Claire a fright. Claire would probably call the police if she saw him pull up in front of her new house. When her lawyer called about the divorce he assured Dave that she meant to make no claim against the assets of the Auk, would in fact deny having had anything to do with the place. No doubt she was worried that an association with the bizarre episode would seriously damage her Washington prospects.

He drove from the Victoria Hotel (CSIS had spared no expense) west to the waterfront. Passing the ships at their moorings, he resisted blowing the horn just for the sake of the noise.

From the waterfront he took the machine up Signal Hill. In the parking lot below Cabot Tower he swung the truck in a big circle. The city below and then the ocean filled the windshield. A fog bank, a great puffy wall, was closing in on the harbor, the autumn sun lacking the power to burn it off. He didn't stop but turned straight back down the hill. If he didn't soon head for the Auk he would be late and they had been very particular over the time he should arrive and clear out his belongings. Dave knew they didn't like him much.

Dave figured he embarrassed them, guessed that higher-ups had scolded Partington's group for having mounted such an elaborate operation only to apprehend an eccentric restaurateur, have one man taken hostage, another two hospitalized and a civilian killed. And still they didn't have the precious Svetkov lamps.

Big horse chestnuts made a canopy over Empire Avenue. St. John's looked stunning this time of year, looked newer in the fall than in the spring. The city knew how to die gracefully. Dave turned the truck on to King's Bridge Road and started north for Push Cove.

During his lengthy interrogation Dave told them that there were other lamps in the tunnel, but a search turned up nothing. Phonse evidently had snatched the tunnel lamps during his flight. To give them their prize would have been admitting defeat. Perhaps he meant to use them as a bargaining tool. It was a mystery. Dave told them that they likely had only to offer Phonse a cash settlement and protection from the Winnebago Corporation and they would have had their precious lights. As it stood, the lamps from the tunnel were probably at the bottom of Push Cove with the collapsed remains of the R.S.V., a trophy for Davy Jones. They told Dave that an explosion had blown a hole in the side of the little submarine and that the resultant change in water pressure crushed it flat like an empty beer can.

They volunteered other details that now meant very little to Dave. Lest any part of the bungled operation become public, they seized the round man's camera and thus the only good photographic record of the decoy. They later told Dave that the man's camera, minus its exposed film, was returned with six new rolls of film in compensation. They told him that Phonse had likely been right in his speculation that Uri Svetkov was living under another name in California. They told him that Claire, the Round Man, Alice and Debbie had all signed undertakings like himself never to discuss the events of that fateful night. If Dave violated the undertaking they would deal with him harshly. If the matter became public they would have no reason not to press charges of forcible confinement, assault and even treason. It was laughable, really.

The truck was on the double highway now, the stretch the locals called the Torbay 500 because it afforded such a wonderful opportunity to speed. The truck had some guts, Dave thought. Why not take the big road trip? His calendar was empty.

What they had not told Dave was why the Svetkov lamps were of such interest. He asked and received only cold stares in response, as if they thought Dave knew the lights' function and was only being coy.

He turned off the highway and on to the Upper Road.

As he passed the car wreckers' bungalows a giant, snarling German shepherd came at the truck. Dave looked in the rearview mirror. He saw the dog lie down in the middle of the road, lacking the motivation to live.

He could see the spire of St. Clare of Assisi Church down in Push Through. Phonse's memorial service had been held there. The little church had been packed. The Upper Road crowd, all in ill-fitting suits, attended and were surprisingly grief-stricken. There was a contingent from the navy, older officers in white uniforms with high collars. Phonse never told Dave that he had served and even been decorated. Valor.

The service was awkward for Dave. He sat next to Alice, who, in a tapered black dress and black lace stockings, elicited a profound aching erection in him. He could not turn his thoughts to his late friend and had to keep squirming in the pew to stop his cock from making an embarrassing tent of his trousers.

The parish priest, Father Furlong, had never liked Phonse, a fact that was reflected in his choice of Scripture. The priest read from Job. Dave could still remember it.

When I looked for good, then evil came unto me: and when I waited for light, there came darkness. My bowels boiled, and rested not: the days of affliction prevented me.

I went mourning without the sun:

I stood up, and I cried in the congregation.

I am a brother to dragons, and a companion to owls.

My skin is black upon me, and my bones are burned with heat.

My harp also is turned to mourning, and my organ into the voice of them that weep.

After the service Dave found Debbie to be handling her loss exceptionally well. She assured Dave that Phonse was probably happier where he was.

Outside the church he invited Alice back to his hotel, but she had a plane to catch, an interview at The Canadian Centre for Architecture in Montreal. In the days Dave was being interrogated, news came that she had been accepted to some program of study of the photographs that so interested her. Dave wondered whether she felt betrayed because he had not told her of the shenanigans he and Phonse were up to, but she kissed him firmly on the lips in parting and insisted that he get to Montreal quickly. Perhaps he would. He didn't even have a Plan A.

There was a chain across the drive leading down to the Auk and a sign posted reading Under Renovations. Dave was about to get out to look for someone when a body emerged from the bushes to remove the chain, letting the truck pass. They had warned him there would be guards on the Auk, necessary since the intrusion of a group of paleontologists, who were reported to have made a startling fossil discovery in the area.

He turned the truck around in the parking lot and backed it up to the Auk's front door. It was their building now, having agreed to Dave's inflated original offer. They seemed so cavalier with the bucks that Dave asked them to pay for the truck rental. This was curtly refused.

The claim of new ownership and renovations was simply a screen to conceal efforts to retrieve the remains of the

R.S.V. in the hope of finding even fragments of the Svetkov lamps. "They must be some kind of lamps," Dave had said. They said nothing.

Their belief that they would somehow keep their salvage operation from the prying eyes of Push Through was a joke, but Dave kept quiet.

The kitchen at the Auk was eerily still. The silver, copper and steel had dulled, mold had appeared in a half-empty wine glass on the counter, the onions and garlic had sprouted long green tendrils, the room smelled of ferment and rot. The hundred candles with which Alice had lit the room all those weeks ago had melted and run off their saucers in waxy strings. Wax stalactites hung from the bar. The Auk had the unsettling air of a project abruptly and inexplicably abandoned, a *Marie Celeste*.

Dave packed only a single suitcase with clothes.

Despite arriving at nine in the morning he didn't finish filling the truck with his wines (in which he had lost interest), the best of the kitchen equipment, a few choice books and the stereo system until almost seven in the evening.

He took a last stroll down the trail to the sea. It was late September, the most beautiful time of the year in Newfoundland. The stands of green spruce were now decorated with flashes of mustard and saffron, autumn birch and alder and sumach. The air was a cordial, sweetly scented by ripe berries, wanting to be drunk.

He had a smoke on the beach and surveyed the water of Push Cove, the still, perfect, blue sheet.

He had not told the people from CSIS about the little

cave on the other side of the cove. He was curious about the punt Phonse used to return from the hideaway. If it was not tied up over there, then . . .

He saw a flock of geese fly overhead, beginning the move south. He heard a chickadee sing to the setting sun. The caper and its consequences had attuned Dave to the wing. Reading a racing shadow, his eyes turned skyward, noting an eagle. His ears registered trill whistles and percussive clicks, the clucks and croaks that crows know. For Dave Purcell the atmosphere was now, and would forever be, filled with music.

Ducks were on the water of Push Cove too, taking their last sustenance before joining the geese and leaving the punishing Newfoundland winter behind.

Dave walked up the hill and back to his rented truck, failing to notice among the other ducks on the water that day a particular bird, a bird with its wing lifted, its head tucked underneath, preening itself purposefully, a little dandy, a peculiar bird, a wildly colored bird with a ridiculous white tuft on its head. A rare bird.

About the Author

A noted writer for the stage, screen and radio, Edward Riche wrote the feature film *Secret Nation* and the stage plays *Possible Maps* and *List of Lights*. Other projects include CBC Radio's "The Great Eastern" and scripts for the television comedy, "Made in Canada," as well as the screenplay for *Rare Birds*. Edward Riche lives in St. John's, Newfoundland. *Rare Birds* is his first novel.